This book is dedicated to doing common things in uncommon ways.

Chapter 1

The week before the end of the academic term, the whole school gathered for the evaluation of students' grades. Louisa Secondary School was a Catholic boarding school which had a culture of holding assemblies right after final exams were graded. These assemblies were nicknamed "deadly assemblies" because students who had failed core classes were flogged by their teachers in front of the whole school. Deadly assemblies were supposedly incorporated to instill fear in poorly performing students to motivate them to work harder. They were called "deadly" because the humiliation could break a student's spirit. The suspense leading up to the assembly was particularly excruciating because students were only allowed to see their grades after the assembly. As a student, all you could do was hope that you hadn't failed a core class. After the assembly, class teachers would then paste spreadsheets of their students' grades and rankings on the entrance doors of each classroom. This lack of confidentiality for students' grades created an unhealthy competition among them. Students who performed poorly were mocked in the dormitories by their high-performing peers and nosy non-classmates who passed by other classes to peep at their class rankings. Sadly, students who were constantly ridiculed for their grades gradually developed low self-esteem which affected their mental health throughout the rest of their secondary school experience.

Udoka was a top student popularly known as the "teachers' pet." Although brilliant, her good grades never stopped her from feeling anxious whenever deadly assemblies were to be held. She was humble by nature and never assumed she was above failing an exam. Her humility was probably what made her put in so much effort into her studies. Her anxiety was geared not only towards herself, but also towards her best friend, Aina. Aina was one of the kindest human beings Udoka had ever met. Udoka nicknamed her "Saintly Aina" because she imitated the behavior of the saints who were portrayed in the Catholic catechism classes which Udoka attended regularly. Although Aina had the perfect personality, she struggled terribly in her studies. She performed poorly in both qualitative and quantitative reasoning and was always at the bottom of her class rankings for midterms and final exams. Aina was only able to pass the entrance exam to Louisa Secondary School because she had attended an educationally inclusive primary school in Nigeria called American Elementary School of Lagos (AESL), which effectively prepared her academically on a primary level despite her scholastic shortcomings. The school's policy was less concerned about students' rankings and more focused on helping each child learn at their own pace and in their own unique style.

In her first grade at AESL, Aina was diagnosed with dyslexia. Dyslexia was described as a learning disorder commonly known to cause difficulty in reading due to poor ability to identify speech sounds and how they related to letters and words. Dyslexia could also cause difficulty in understanding numbers and math concepts. Fortunately, AESL was renowned for making accommodations for students with learning disabilities. The most common learning disability was dyslexia. To support students with this problem, it ensured that all its class teachers were well trained on the Orton-Gillingham approach. This approach focused on non-traditional ways to teach dyslexic students how to sort, recognize, and organize the raw materials for thinking and use. Unfortunately, after Aina graduated from AESL, her parents could not find a secondary school in Nigeria that operated based on the same inclusive educational policy.

Udoka tried tutoring Aina during leisure hours, but it was all in vain. Aina ended up repeating Junior Secondary School One (JSS1) three times and eventually was instructed to transfer to a different school. She wasn't meeting the academic standards of Louisa Secondary School. When Aina was set to leave Louisa Secondary School, Udoka was already in Junior Secondary School Three (JSS3) and was about to take her Junior School Certificate Examination (JSCE) exam. Unsure of the next time they would reunite, she cherished their last days together in school. After Aina left, Udoka spent her final three years in secondary school wondering why someone like Aina with such a beautiful soul could be so disadvantaged academically. To Udoka, life seemed so unfair. Little did she know that Aina had her own life treasure waiting for her ahead.

Aina, not being able to excel in any Nigerian secondary school, eventually moved to America to get a special needs middle school and high school education. She was adopted by her aunt to help her gain citizenship. Aina enrolled into a school which made accommodations for students with dyslexia and began to improve academically. Although she improved in math and literacy, she never got the best grades in these classes. She was mostly a "C" student when it came to these subjects, earning a few "B" grades sometimes. While Aina navigated adolescence, she became increasingly self-conscious about her dyslexia. Although she had enrolled into a new school, she was still dealing with post-traumatic stress disorder (PTSD) from her time at Louisa Secondary School. Her PTSD manifested in the form of nightmares, anxiety, and depression. Also, the more "C" grades she got in math and literacy, the more her self-esteem began to drop. She was reluctant to accept that even with her learning accommodations, being dyslexic meant that she might never be a top student in math and literacy.

Aina's aunt, being aware of her depression, enrolled her in therapy. Fortunately, as time went by, not only did therapy help Aina learn about self-acceptance, but it also helped her see herself in a new light. During one of her discussions with her therapist about her hobbies, she realized that she was highly skilled in fine arts, mainly painting and pattern designing. She performed exceptionally in her art classes at school and was always complimented by her art teachers. Before then, coming from a Nigerian school where little or no recognition was given for excellence in fine arts, she had developed the flawed idea that true intelligence was measured only in math and literacy. Her therapist introduced her to Leonardo da Vinci, a historical figure who although was dyslexic, was remembered for his innovative techniques in art, entrepreneurship, among other things. Aina, with help from her therapist, developed confidence in herself and her artistic abilities. To follow in Leonardo da Vinci's footsteps, she thought about pursuing art and entrepreneurship as a long-term career. She knew that she was great at painting and pattern designing, but soon realized that there was not a huge market for painters. She then thought about what lucrative career would merge pattern designing with entrepreneurship and decided that fashion entrepreneurship was a plausible route.

      Aina's choice to take on fashion entrepreneurship came at the right time when she was starting to realize that she had an eccentric sense of style. She loved artsy outfits and accessories that weren't ubiquitous. Unfortunately, she couldn't find many affordable clothing lines that appealed to her fashion taste. In response to this problem, she had always dreamed of making her own outlandish clothes and accessories. In her leisure time, she would design distinctive textile patterns on adobe photoshop and illustrator and imagine herself strutting in clothes embodying these designs. After doing extensive research on Leonardo da Vinci's unique contribution to entrepreneurship and art, she was inspired to launch a business in eccentric fashion. She wanted to make quirky affordable clothes for herself and other people who had her sense of style. Aina's aunt wanted her to focus on completing high school first, but Aina disagreed. She believed that she could go to school and simultaneously pursue entrepreneurship. She insisted that school was preparing her primarily in math and literacy needed for traditional careers which she was unlikely to excel in because of her dyslexia. Hence, the smart thing to do was to start early to explore a career route such as entrepreneurship, which she knew she could excel in. She highlighted that most dyslexic people succeeded as entrepreneurs because of their highly visual and creative minds. She finally changed her aunt's mind by telling a story of a young African American boy and entrepreneur, Moziah Bridges, about Aina's age, who with his mother, appeared on Shark Tank, one of her favorite television shows.

Moziah loved wearing bow ties but couldn't find affordable fashionable bow ties. He then decided to make his bow ties himself. With some help from his grandmother and mother, he began to make high quality bow ties with beautiful patterns. Although he enjoyed wearing his new fashionable bow ties, he also thought about launching a business out of it. His mother and grandmother supported him by making enough bow ties to sell on Etsy, an ecommerce website. While his bow tie business grew, Moziah remained a full-time student. To expand the business and get an investor, Moziah and his mother pitched his business idea on Shark Tank and eventually got Daymond John as a mentor. Daymond John was popularly known as the founder, president, and chief executive officer of FUBU, a successful American hip hop fashion clothing brand. He was a prominent investor on Shark Tank and the only African American investor on the show. Shark Tank was an American television reality show about five investors who competed to invest in or reject the ideas of entrepreneurs who came on the show to pitch their ideas. Every entrepreneur had the hope of growing their business with the expertise and investment of one or more sharks. Daymond John chose to mentor Moziah Bridges because he saw himself in him. Like Moziah, Daymond, at a young age, ventured into fashion to create unique clothes that represented African American culture. He launched FUBU (For Us, By Us), a company which was founded on the same principles as Moziah's company, Mo's Bows. With mentorship from Daymond John, Moziah grew his company successfully enough to turn him into a millionaire at just age seventeen.

Aina's aunt, moved by Moziah's story, decided to support Aina in her new fashion venture. Fortunately, she had seamstress skills, enabling her to teach Aina how to sew her first set of outfits. Aina began designing unique textile patterns which were mainly abstract forms of African symbols such as Adinkra. Adinkra were symbols believed to be originally created by the Asante (Ashanti) craftsmen of Ghana. They were designed to portray the culture of these artisans. Aina successfully transferred her textile patterns onto good quality cotton fabrics at a nearby screen printing company and began the sewing process. After school and on weekends, Aina kept busy sewing her unconventional outfits. Soon, she began wearing these outfits to school, social events, church, the mall, and anywhere she could get people to notice her unique style. As she had hoped, people noticed her and inquired about where she had purchased the outfits. In response, she informed them that she had designed the patterns and sewed the clothes herself. Everyone who heard her story was astonished. How could a teenager be so talented? They all wanted a taste of her fashion. Aina had managed to make quirky fashion look cool in her community. She eventually opened a shop on Etsy to sell some of her clothes. Orders started to pour in, and in response, Aina had to increase inventory.

To grow her business, she convinced her aunt to take out loans on her behalf. She then rented a space near her home and began looking to hire tailors to sew outfits suited to customers' orders. Her aunt, who was a social worker assisting female survivors of sex trafficking, pleaded with Aina to hire these clients who were desperately in need of income. Aina agreed. Upon getting to know her aunt's clients whom she had agreed to hire, Aina learned that before eventually escaping, most of them had gotten into sex slavery by being kidnapped by traffickers, or by being sold by their parents to traffickers to help with the family income or to pay off family debts. Aina willingly employed these women, trained them, and paid them enough to help them afford decent homes. As fate would have it, after applying three times to pitch her business idea on Shark Tank, she was finally invited to the tank. Daymond John upon meeting her, was fascinated by her story and indicated how she reminded him of Moziah Bridges, one of his mentees. However, instead of simply choosing to mentor Aina like he had done with Moziah, he decided to invest in her business for a twenty percent stake. Being the founder of FUBU, fashion was his forte, and more importantly, he liked Aina's profit margin. They ended up being excellent business partners over the next few years. They also bonded over the fact that they were both dyslexics. Daymond brought in the money, network, and expansion strategies, while Aina brought in more unique pattern designs and skilled labor. The business was flourishing and expanding so much that Wall Street Journal invited Aina for an interview.

During the interview, she told a story about how back in Nigeria, she had struggled in school with dyslexia and eventually had to move to America to pursue special needs education because no Nigerian secondary school would accommodate her. She highlighted how her quirkiness was the soul of her fashion brand which she named "Oyatosi" meaning "different" in Yoruba, her native Nigerian tongue. She also noted that a huge percentage of her employees were survivors of sex trafficking who desperately needed income to reintegrate into the society. Aina's story warmed the hearts of many Americans and people all over the world. Many parents forced their kids to read her story to imbibe her summary message, "Be comfortable in your own skin. The world has a place for you." By employing survivors of sex trafficking, she started a national and soon to be global movement to help sex trafficking survivors reintegrate into the society.

Aina, who was still the sole designer of patterns for her business, could no longer keep up with the rapidly expanding business orders. Hence, she put out adverts to hire co-designers who were skilled in creating outlandish clothing patterns. Aina and her team interviewed the job applicants and reviewed their design samples before selecting the best ten to be her co-designers. She then expanded into various American cities specifically known for high rates of sex trafficking. In no time, Oyatosi had become a national social justice fashion brand. In addition to clothing, Aina also printed her patterns on accessories such as shoes, bags, socks, etc., and interior design items such as wallpapers, carpets, pillowcases, couch covers, bedsheets, etc.

Aina graduated from high school and continued with entrepreneurship full-time. After years of successfully running her clothing brand, she decided to venture into investing. She had been a huge fan of Shark Tank where she had met her business partner who was an investor on the show. However, instead of applying to become a shark on Shark Tank, she decided to create her own show, like Shark Tank, called "Tiger's Den," in Nigeria. Being well-known globally for her fashion brand, she was easily able to connect and partner with people in the television space in Nigeria who were eager to be associated with her. She hired four other experienced investors to be her co-tigers, and the show was launched. It became a major hit, first in Lagos, then other states in Nigeria. Eventually, news spread to other African countries. It was launched on African television stations before moving to Netflix. As soon as it hit Netflix, the show's popularity became global. Aina had become a successful fashion entrepreneur, an investor in African businesses, and the founder and producer of a Nigerian reality television series. She was clearly headed towards billionaire status by age thirty.

Aina, being aware of her huge success in Nigeria, wanted to give back to the community. She eventually settled on philanthropy in dyslexia interventions. She was disappointed that the Nigerian Ministry of Education still had not begun addressing learning disabilities in Nigerian schools. To address this problem, she traveled to the most popular primary and secondary schools in Lagos to discuss the possibility of initiating dyslexia interventions within their curriculum. She was willing to fund the training of teachers on the Orton-Gillingham approach. The training would be carried out by international dyslexia specialists whom she had employed to partner with her. Most of the schools agreed to the partnership, and her program, Embracing Dyslexia, was immediately launched. Each partnering school was first required to screen all their students for dyslexia using a universal screening test. The success of the program was then measured based on the improvement of these students on academic tests after a year of undergoing the Orton-Gillingham approach. The partnering schools periodically sent their statistics to her team. After three years of evaluating the effectiveness of the program, she was confident enough to approach the Nigerian Ministry of Education with her positive results.

With the bureaucracy in the Nigerian government, the Nigerian Ministry of Education was sluggish to adopt her efforts. Frustrated, Aina resorted towards activism. She made adverts on television and radio stations about dyslexia and called out the Nigerian Ministry of Education's reluctance to address learning disabilities in Nigerian schools. She called on higher education schools to ensure that their teachers-in-training were mandated to take at least one course in dyslexia before graduating. She also highlighted the success of the Embracing Dyslexia program and called on the elite to donate towards the cause. She called on students within her program as well as Nigerians interested in her cause to initiate street protests. She also pleaded with Nigerian schools to abolish the public display of students' grades and rankings to protect the self-esteem of these students. She called on Nigerian exam boards such as NECO and JAMB to include an option of oral testing for dyslexic students who were more likely to perform better in oral than written exams.

After months of protests and media campaigns, Aina started to see some changes. She got large donations from wealthy Lagos families including the Otedolas, Dangotes, Adenugas, Elumelus, Alakijas, and many others. More Nigerian schools reached out to partner with her team on initiating training for their teachers. Aina was busier than ever with running her entrepreneurial businesses as well as the Embracing Dyslexia program, but she was the most fulfilled she had ever been. She had achieved financial freedom for herself while also creating social impact.

Chapter 2

In her final year at Louisa Secondary School, Udoka sat for the West African Senior School Certificate Examination (WASSCE). WASSCE was a standardized test in West Africa, administered by the West African Examinations Council (WAEC). Students who passed the exam received a certificate confirming their graduation from secondary education. Udoka passed with the highest grades and was ranked third position in Nigeria out of 1.7 million students who took the examination. WAEC awarded the top three students with monetary compensation which Udoka happily deposited in a bank. As the first at her secondary school to win such an award, she was celebrated in the school's hall of fame. Owing to her achievements, people began to wonder whether Udoka was going to enroll at a university in Nigeria or abroad. She eventually opted to go to school in the United States (U.S.).

Coincidentally, around that same time, Udoka's mother won a U.S. visa lottery and was granted an opportunity to apply for permanent residency. The application emerged successful which meant that she had become lawfully permitted to live permanently in the U.S. She was also allowed to apply to bring Udoka over as a dependent, since she was a minor. Udoka, being the only child of her parents, moved to the U.S. to be with her mother, and began to apply to U.S. colleges. Udoka's father chose to remain in Southeastern Nigeria, Anambra state, to keep running the fish farm and supermarket which he inherited from his grandfather. He habitually spoke negatively of western culture, rejecting every idea of settling there with his family. He loved his hometown, Nimo, especially because most of his friends were there. Udoka's parents decided that Udoka's mother would visit her husband every year once she found a well-paying job in America.

Life began for Udoka and her mother in America. Leveraging her experience as a former vice principal of an elementary school in Nigeria, Udoka's mother was able to get a substitute teaching job to begin her teaching career in America. She was told that she could only work as a substitute teacher until she had passed the exams that certified her to teach in America. Unfortunately, these exams were administered within a span of one year at different intervals. Missing one exam could set you back for months. Sadly, Udoka's mother fell ill with pneumonia a night before an exam, causing her to postpone it. This impromptu occurrence elongated the time it took for her to become a certified teacher. She continued with her substitute teaching job while Udoka kept applying to colleges that were generous with scholarships. She and her mother lived in a one-bedroom apartment in a semi-safe neighborhood in Houston, Texas.

Calamity struck again when the U.S. suddenly began to experience an economic recession, leading many businesses to lay off employees. Unfortunately, Udoka's mother was one of those laid off. For months, she couldn't find another teaching job because she still had not completed her certificate exams. Udoka, desperate to contribute financially to the family's upkeep, paused enrolling into college. Her mother thought about moving back to Nigeria for a while but as a permanent resident, she was required to live in the U.S. for a minimum of five years before her status could transition into U.S. citizenship. Hence, she and Udoka, unwilling to jeopardize their path to citizenship, decided to remain in the U.S. to fight the recession. Being a teenager in a recession made it hard for Udoka to find a job, but she and her mother were relentless. As her mother's savings kept diminishing fast, Udoka reluctantly decided to consider fashion modeling for the second time. Her first time had been back in Nigeria when she had taken on short-term modeling jobs during school breaks.

Udoka was not a fan of the modeling industry because of its influence in pressuring women to adopt the popular skinny body type. To get skinny enough for runway shows and photoshoots, some female models typically became either anorexic or bulimic. Udoka became a victim of anorexia in Nigeria when she ventured into modeling back in senior secondary school two (SSS2). She enjoyed partaking in runway shows and photoshoots for budding designers but hated the toll it took on her mental image of herself. She became so skinny and unhealthy that her mother had to pull her out of modeling. Udoka's mother, scared of her daughter's alarmingly low body mass index, began to feed her pounded yam and different native soups until she regained her healthy weight. This incident marked the end of modeling for Udoka in Nigeria. In addition to causing poor eating habits, Udoka's mother hated the modeling industry for encouraging indecent dressing. However, Udoka debated the topic of indecency in dressing with her mother, explaining that many years ago, before western colonization, African women used to move around topless or simply tied wrappers below their breasts. Also, their skirts were typically short enough to cover only their private parts. Western colonization was what made them ashamed of their bodies.

"We were all born naked, so as adults, why can't we walk around naked if we want to? What if the weather is so hot and I don't want to put on any clothes? Why shame me?" mentioned Udoka, further buttressing her point. "It's Adam and Eve's fault. They disobeyed God and ate the apple and then became aware of their nakedness, and then had to cover their bodies," responded her mother. "Okay, but did the Bible specify what parts of their bodies they covered?" asked Udoka. Her mother giggled and responded, "I'm not sure. I think the Catholic church is against nudity based on "intent" in the sense that you shouldn't show skin to seduce anybody. That's when it becomes a sin. Also, look at my phone cover. What is its function? It serves to protect my phone, right? Your clothes are meant to protect your skin." "Good point, but what if I don't want to protect my skin or seduce anybody? What if I just enjoy being naked? Should it be anybody's business? Why should the police arrest me for nudity?" queried Udoka.

Understanding that desperate times called for desperate measures, her mother finally agreed to her trying out modeling again as long as she maintained a healthy weight. To launch her U.S. modelling career, Udoka found a photographer who was looking to build his portfolio.

She struck a deal with him entailing that with her beautiful body and face, if she were to agree to model for him, he would have to give her copies of the pictures for free. She then used these copies to build her portfolio and apply for modeling jobs. Unfortunately, multiple modeling agencies loved her photos but found her to be too short. She was five feet seven inches, but unluckily, they typically took models who were five feet nine inches and above. Udoka, however, was relentless and decided to try freelance modeling. One day, she found an advertisement in a newspaper stating that models were needed for a fashion show and video shoot in Los Angeles, California. They wanted slim and beautiful models who were five feet seven inches and above. Udoka was ecstatic and instantly sent her portfolio to the email listed on the advert. The next day, she received a response stating that she was going to be flown to Los Angeles for the casting and training.

  Being nineteen years old going on twenty, Udoka's mother was convinced that she was old enough to travel alone. Her mother, who was financially setback, couldn't afford to purchase a flight ticket to accompany her to California. Unfortunately, the modeling agency was only willing to cover the travel expenses of solely the incoming model. Udoka packed her bags, after which her mother drove her to the airport. Udoka's mother bade her daughter farewell, expecting her to be back in one week with enough money to take care of them for some months before the next gig. Sadly, her daughter never returned the next week. She called Udoka's phone continuously, but it had been disconnected. She did not see her child for the next five years.

Chapter 3

When Udoka arrived in Los Angeles at the casting site, she was asked to ride with the other models in a black van with tinted windows. All the models were dressed similarly in white tank tops, skinny jeans, and stiletto heels. Every girl was slim, somewhat tall, and young-looking, probably in their teenage years or early twenties. Udoka blended in well. The girls were told that they would be transported to a different site where they would be screened for the upcoming runway shows, video shoots, and photo shoots that week. They were all excited and ready to embark on the road trip.

Udoka found the trip longer than she had anticipated. She had taken a nap, woken up, eaten some snacks provided by the agents, used the in-built bathroom on the van twice, and they still had not reached their destination. They had begun the trip in the afternoon and had still not arrived by evening time. Finally, the van pulled over in the middle of nowhere. The sky was pitch black by then. The door opened, and eight hostile-looking armed men stood outside, peering into the van. Udoka knew immediately that something was wrong. Growing up Catholic, she began to recite the Rosary in her head, invoking the Holy Spirit to protect her.

The models were each handcuffed and led forcefully to a building with multiple floors. Each floor consisted of many cells like prison cells that Udoka had seen in movies. Her heart started to pound. She knew she had been kidnapped. She wanted to call her mother desperately. Where was her phone? She then remembered that the agents had seized all their belongings. There was no way out. She was shoved into a cell by two muscular men, alongside another model who would become her cellmate. The men uncuffed the girls and instructed them to remain in their cells till further notice. Her cellmate soon began to weep uncontrollably. Udoka simply stared at her, not knowing how to respond. She too was in a state of shock.

Eventually, the guards reappeared and handcuffed the two girls again, leading them to a private room at the end of the hallway. They were about to undergo "seasoning," a term used to describe the raping and beating of newly trafficked girls to break their bodies, souls, and spirits in preparation for their jobs as sex slaves. This act was believed to make them submissive. Udoka and her roommate were beat up and raped by ten different men before being dumped back into their cells. The rape was particularly more painful for Udoka because she had been a virgin, and it hurt profusely to be penetrated so violently without a lubricant. Udoka could not sleep that night. Her whole body hurt. She cursed the day she was born. Her cellmate tried to strangle herself multiple times with her bare hands but failed.

Morning came, and the armed guards appeared again to give the girls bathing towels, toiletries, a few casual tops and shorts, flip flops, blankets, a couple of seductive and over-revealing short dresses, and each a pair of stiletto heels that matched their shoe sizes. They were each given a manual that read:

DAILY SCHEDULE OF EMPLOYEE

7: 00 am: Wake up. Do morning chores. Do laundry. Clean up the cells, hallways, and bathrooms. A schedule should be created by the employees on each hallway to take turns to clean their hallway and bathrooms and do laundry for everyone in their section. Each employee will have their name sewn on a small tag on each clothing material and towel to enable easy identification.

8: 00 am: Shower and prepare for work. Employees must wear seductive outfits and must be in at least 5-inch heels. Thighs and cleavages must be exposed.

9: 00 am: Proceed to the dining hall for breakfast.

9: 30 am: Proceed to the brothel to meet with clients.

1: 00 pm: Proceed to the dining hall for lunch.

1: 30 pm: Return to the brothel.

6: 00 pm: Proceed to the dining hall for dinner.

6: 30 pm: Return to the brothel.

9: 00 pm: Employee must return to her cell to prepare to shower for the night.

10: 00pm: Lights out.

- Under no circumstances should an employee be fed after 7pm. This will enable her to maintain a slim and sexy figure for the clients.

- If an employee tries to run away, she should be shot in the foot and will be treated later by an on-call doctor.

- If an employee tries to assault another employee, she should be beaten by a guard.

- If an employee tries to assault a client, she should be beaten and starved for two days.

- If an employee tries to assault a guard, she should be beaten by the guard.

- Cells will be inspected at random times to ensure that no employee has any harmful objects that could be used to commit suicide or assault another person.

- No employee is allowed to take money from a client. Any payment for their services will be sent to the brothel manager. Every employee will be searched after work hours for money and foreign objects before returning to their cells.

- A panic button will be placed in every brothel room for an employee to call for help if assaulted by a client.

- Winter operations will be the same as summer operations. The employee should not worry about the cold because the buildings will be heated during the winter. The employee is still required to wear skimpy clothes in the winter to see clients.

- The employee will only be allowed to go outside in handcuffs once a month for thirty minutes to catch fresh air. The rest of the months will be spent moving from their cell to the brothel which are connected via different hallways.

- All clients have been instructed to use condoms when having penetrative sex with an employee.

- The employee will do blood tests every month to check for sexually transmitted diseases (STDs). She will be treated for curable STDs and will be killed and cremated in a nearby incinerator if found to have HIV/AIDS. Hence, she needs to ensure that clients use condoms. If a client refuses to use condoms, she needs to press the panic button in her room and a guard will come to her rescue.

- If an employee gets pregnant, she will be given the option to abort the baby or keep the pregnancy. If she chooses to keep the pregnancy, her baby will be taken from her once it's born.

- The employee should forward any questions she has to the guard on duty.

The girls were told that they had three days to settle in and get ready to obey the manual strictly. Within those three days, the girls underwent "seasoning," while food was brought to their cells at random times. They were also allowed to interact with other employees on their floors to figure out the schedule for the chores.

Udoka began meeting clients on the fifth day of her arrival. Each client, before stopping by the brothel, was allowed access to a catalogue of the prostitutes on duty. The client would then select the photos of their favorite prostitutes and then make online payments to the manager. Her first client was a tall White man with a long beard, which he stroked repeatedly, as he sized her up before pouncing on her. She felt disgusted with herself throughout the first month, but eventually found a way to mentally separate her acts of prostitution from her sense of self-worth. She got better each day at compartmentalizing her feelings.

Over the course of her years as a sex slave, she met a variety of men of different races with distinct personalities. Some were just there to have sex and leave. Some wanted to cuddle up for a few minutes before leaving. Some caught feelings after sex, and wanted to take her home with them, but the guard would not let them. Some spent half the time they paid for, ranting about how their marriages were failing; how their wives had gotten fat after having babies; how their wives had become bad in bed, and refused to give them "blow jobs"; among other personal problems. Udoka looked forward to these talkative clients. Whenever they began ranting, she would pretend to listen, nod, and acknowledge their feelings. She feigned this demeanor to make them feel seen and heard while secretly using the time to cool off her vagina from having nonstop sex with previous clients. Occasionally, she would entertain clients who wanted only oral sex. Sadly, she also received violent clients who would try to choke her, but luckily, she was usually fast enough to press the panic button beside her bed for a guard to come to her rescue. The client would then be dragged out and banned from returning to the brothel. She also had a few female clients who wanted to use sex toys on her. She agreed to their demands if they were willing to wrap condoms on the sex toys before penetrating her with them. Some clients requested BDSM, and Udoka submitted to their wants.

Once, Udoka got pregnant by a client whose condom broke. Being raised Catholic, she was taught to regard abortion as a sin. Hence, she chose to keep the pregnancy. She still adhered to her old schedule except that she stopped being requested by most of her clients once her belly began to expand. However, a few clients were aroused by the idea of *screwing* a pregnant woman, hence, she catered to their services throughout her pregnancy. The day she gave birth to her baby boy, before handing him over to an agent, she invoked the Holy Spirit to protect him wherever he went. Udoka wept continuously that night and was given a week off for her body to recover from childbirth. During that week, she remained in her cell while food was brought to her.

Udoka thought about her mother regularly, and would cry at night, praying to God that her mother had found a job and was living comfortably. Her mother on the other hand had not given up on looking for her child. On the first day of January and July every year, throughout the five years that Udoka was missing, Udoka's mother would show up at a police station to file a missing person report, giving the exact details about how she had lost her child.

One strange night, Udoka woke up in her cell to ongoing sounds of police sirens and helicopter sounds. Then came in numerous FBI agents bursting into the hallways and arresting the guards on duty. Shots were fired, and some resisting guards were killed. Every girl woke up panicking. The police then told the girls to pack their bags, explaining that they were being transported to a safe place. All the girls, about a hundred of them, were led outside into some vans while journalists tried to get in quick interviews about the operations of such horrific sex slavery. The FBI agents accompanied the rescued girls to safe apartments hours away from the brothel. While the girls settled into the apartments, volunteer nurses checked their health statuses, and the FBI began tracking down their relatives. When they got to Udoka, she told them she was from Houston, Texas. They then informed her that her mother had filed a missing person report on her every six months for the last five years. They called her mother on the phone to inform her of Udoka's whereabouts. Over the phone, her mother remained speechless for about two minutes before garnering up the courage to speak to her daughter. She agreed to pick Udoka up from the airport the next day. The flight ticket was covered by a non-profit organization dedicated towards supporting survivors of sex trafficking. Once Udoka saw her mother, she ran and hugged her tightly for nearly five minutes without letting go.

Udoka's mother took her home, prepared her favorite meal, pounded yam and ogbono soup, and watched her intensely as she ate. Udoka told her mother every single detail about her horrendous experience as a sex slave. She spoke about how she was kidnapped and highlighted her sexual encounters with the different clients. Her mother cringed and cried continuously as her child gave explicit descriptions of the sexual acts she had performed on these clients. Udoka and her mother eventually learned that the police had found her because an FBI agent posed as a wealthy VIP client for the trafficking ring for a year while garnering up enough evidence to launch an arrest. As a VIP client, he had to pay huge sums of money to gain access to intimate operations of the trafficking ring and brothel. An investigation into the trafficking ring was launched after multiple parents reported their children missing after supposedly attending a modeling casting in Los Angeles, like Udoka's story.

Udoka inquired about how her mother had survived financially after she was kidnapped. In response, her mother told a story about how her life had turned around in church on the third Sunday after Udoka went missing. After the church service ended, Udoka's mother knelt before the Blessed Sacrament and wept loudly and uncontrollably until a fellow parishioner had to walk over to comfort her. He was an elderly sharp-looking African American man in his fifties. He inquired about her situation, and she explained how she had lost her teaching job, and that her only child had been kidnapped while trying to make an income for the family. The man was devastated and sat to console Udoka's mother, contemplating how he could help her. While chatting with her for a while, he soon learned that she was once a former teacher and deputy principal back in Nigeria. Impressed with her career expertise, he offered her a job to run his late wife's kindergarten school. Udoka's mother, startled by his kindness, instantly accepted the job offer. The man's wife had died from breast cancer four months before then, leaving him to figure out the operations of the school on his own. He was a managing director at a billion-dollar oil company in Houston, forced to carve out time to manage his late wife's school while looking for a new principal. He was excited that Udoka's mother had served as a deputy principal for five years at a British school in Nigeria. She had the experience of running an educational institute and had already acquired many months of American training as a substitute teacher. She was perfect for the role. This encounter ignited the end of Udoka's mother's financial woes.

Udoka, still suffering from PTSD from being a former sex slave, decided to attend therapy for a year before resuming applying to U.S. universities for college. Coincidentally, that same year, she reconnected with her friend, Aina, from Louisa Secondary School. Some months before their reunion, information about the demolition of the trafficking ring that kidnapped Udoka was published on numerous news outlets. Upon seeing the news, Aina had recognized Udoka when her profile was published as one of the survivors. She immediately began trying to reconnect with her. Being a wealthy celebrity, she had enough money and connections to hire a private investigator to track down Udoka's current address and contact. The two long-lost friends were elated to see each other again. They filled each other in on how their lives had transformed over the years. They were both twenty-seven years old by the time they reconnected. Each of them had experienced life's ups and downs uniquely up to that moment. They hung out every day and couldn't get enough of each other. Although Aina was still running the Tiger's Den television show in Lagos, Nigeria, she traveled continually to the U.S. to monitor her Oyatosi clothing brand, and to visit her aunt who was still a social worker based in Houston. Aina filled Udoka in on her fashion business which was still booming. She even asked Udoka to be a part-time model for one of her new clothing lines. Udoka was overjoyed and happily signed up for photoshoots to model Aina's clothes. She also walked runway shows for Aina, including prestigious shows such as ARISE Fashion Week and New York Fashion Week.

Udoka, remembering her struggle with her height and eating habits in the modeling industry, encouraged Aina to hire models of all body types to push boundaries in beauty standards. Aina willingly incorporated Udoka's advice. Also, to assist aspiring models who were non-U.S.

citizens, she launched a modeling agency that filed for work permits for these models. Udoka was in awe of how successful her friend Aina had become. But most importantly, she was blown away by how generous and welcoming she had become towards people in need in her community and around the world.

      Udoka, upon watching her friend, Aina, succeed in life despite being dyslexic, took an interest in atypical brain development. She decided she wanted to study neuroscience in college. After a year of therapy, she also became fascinated by how the mind worked. She was amazed by how her therapist had helped to transform her perspective on life after surviving trauma. Thus, in addition to neuroscience, she decided she also wanted to study psychology. She proceeded to apply to the best U.S. schools in neuroscience and psychology, and eventually got accepted into Mississippi University on a full scholarship. In her personal statement, she wrote about how surviving the trauma of sex slavery and having a dyslexic best friend had influenced her choice to double major in neuroscience and psychology.

Chapter 4

Udoka moved to Mississippi to begin college. Upon arriving, her first observation of the state was its deep rural and serene culture. She had heard about Mississippi's southern hospitality culture and was excited to experience it. Although impressed with the warm demeanor of strangers, she was not happy with the infrastructure. There was no airport near her school, thus, she had to fly into Memphis International Airport which was in Tennessee. The airport being a two-hour drive from her school, bothered Udoka. Unable to find a bus or train going to her school campus, she resorted to using a taxi which cost her a hundred dollars. Udoka was devastated. She had not budgeted for the high transportation fees. Mississippi's underdeveloped public transportation system took her by surprise.

Udoka eventually got to Mississippi University and moved into her room which was in a residential hall on campus. Her school had made it mandatory for first-year students to live on campus. Udoka spent the first week of school struggling to settle in. She got lost on campus multiple times while trying to find her classes. However, by the third week, life became more stable for her. As a result of pursuing a double major in psychology and neuroscience, Udoka had to take more classes than the usual freshman. She was a lot older and more mature than her classmates, and thus was equipped to handle a more rigorous lifestyle than them. As a nerd, Udoka enjoyed the lifestyle of constant reading of class materials. She loved learning about the brain as well as human behavior.

Through her classes, she found fascinating intersections between neuroscience and psychology. She looked forward more to individual projects than group projects which she found to be increasingly frustrating. Udoka's classes were low in diversity, and as a result, she was frequently the only Black person in team projects. Her classes consisted of mostly White students, a characteristic that Udoka later came to accept upon learning that Mississippi University was a predominantly white institution (PWI). She still had her thick Nigerian accent which scared off some of her classmates. Although she was fluent in English, her classmates were still nervous to engage in long conversations with her. She found herself having to repeat sentences when conversing with them. There was frustration on both ends.

Udoka, not being able to bond with her classmates in her first year, sought friendships outside of class. She joined the African Caribbean Student Association (ACSA) to connect with African and Afro-Caribbean students on campus. She was desperate to connect with Black people. There were a couple of African Americans in some of her classes, but they too, like White students, were reluctant to bond with her. Through bonding over being Black and foreign at Mississippi University, ACSA quickly became Udoka's family.

Udoka's mother frequently called her, insisting that she remained diligent in her Catholic faith. In response to her mother's advice, Udoka became a member of St. Vincent de Paul Catholic Church near her school. Unsurprisingly, the church's parishioners were mostly

White. However, they were much friendlier than her classmates. She joined a Bible study group which met every Sunday evening to discuss scripture readings. As time went by, Udoka grew close to two of its members who were White female upperclassmen. They began to hang out outside of Bible study group meetings. Her new friends, Anna and Lindsay, were in their third year of pursuing undergraduate degrees in business. They were classmates and childhood friends who had decided to help each other build on their Catholic faith. Upon getting to know Udoka, they were excited to have an African friend. Udoka generally enjoyed their genuine curiosity about African culture but soon became frustrated by their relentless ignorant questions. Once, while studying together for midterm exams, they asked her whether Africans knew how to use calculators and laptops, leaving her startled. Udoka also became irritated by their White savior complex. Their first display of this complex occurred when she mentioned that she was Nigerian, but instead of inquiring further about Nigeria, they began to tell her random stories about their missionary trips to Tanzania and Zambia. They then showed her pictures of the huts they had built for members of remote communities in these countries, as well as random photos they had taken with indigent street kids. Although they seemed proud to have "saved" these poor African communities, all Udoka could see from each photo shown to her was a display of poverty porn. How had they suddenly shifted the conversation from talking about Nigeria to discussing their White savior escapades in Tanzania and Zambia? Why had they assumed she knew anything about Tanzania and Zambia? Was this a typical

American way of putting Africans in a box? Udoka, disappointed, congratulated them on their service projects regardless.

Udoka enjoyed weekend outings with her new White friends but soon began to feel like a trophy friend. She noticed that when with other people, they would constantly brag about her being African; they seemed to care more about her ethnicity than about her behavioral traits as a friend. She often wondered if they were just friends with her because she was African. Months into the friendship, Udoka began to pick up on racial microaggressions made by them. Once, when Udoka informed them that she had been admitted into the honors college, they congratulated her, but subtly commented that the honors college probably incorporated affirmative action into their admission process. They basically implied that she had been admitted simply because she was Black. The honors college was a prestigious program for high performing students on campus. Udoka wanted to respond by asserting that her high grade point average (GPA) was what got her into the program, but she resorted to silence. Weeks later, they made another disturbing statement, mentioning that they enjoyed associating with her because she was different from other Black people. Udoka laughed off the comment, but deep down, she was unsettled. Udoka's annoyance grew when they began to ruffle her afro without her permission. Udoka, tired of her usual braids, had decided to wear her afro for a while. Her White friends, never having had Black friends before, were fascinated by the softness and thickness of her afro and proceeded to ruffle it at random times. This act annoyed

Udoka especially because she typically spent a long time every morning getting her afro into a desired shape. She eventually complained to her friends about their overstepping of boundaries, and they apologized. The friendship continued.

During Udoka's second year in college, she noticed that she could no longer complete her tests on time. The tests had become increasingly difficult. Although she typically knew how to solve all the problems, she still commonly needed more time to complete them. She spoke to her professors about this problem and was encouraged to report the issue to the disability office on campus. The disability office first put her through a series of interviews. Next, they confirmed from her professors that she was a diligent and brilliant student who was simply struggling with speed. They then asked her to provide a doctor's report permitting her to get extra time on tests. Udoka set up an appointment at her school's health clinic to get a doctor's report, after which she was granted extra time on tests by the disability office. She was given multiple copies of an official slip stating that each professor was to provide her with twice the amount of time given to students for every exam. With her performance improving as a result, Udoka often wondered if she would have failed out of school had she not been given extra time on tests. She wished Nigerian schools would incorporate this technique into their educational systems.

By the end of her second year in college, Udoka was ready to gain work experience pertaining to her majors. Thus, she applied to psychology and neuroscience consulting firms for internships. Upon receiving multiple offers, she decided to take a year off from school to do four different internships/co-ops with four different firms. She began with a summer internship at a psychology firm where she worked as a counseling/mental health intern. There, she assisted the specialists in the areas of counseling, behavioral health, and addictions. Next, she did a fall co-op at a neuroscience firm as a histology intern. There, she did research on chemical neuroanatomy. After her fall co-op, she did a spring co-op at another psychology firm where she worked as a performance psychology intern. There, she operated under the research department to collect qualitative data and analyses on matters related to mental health and mental performance in professional sports. Finally, she ended her one year of work experience with a summer internship at a neuroscience firm where she did research on childhood developmental disorders. Upon returning to school, Udoka received grades for these internships/co-ops. In addition, her work experiences gave her a broader view of psychology and neuroscience which influenced how she proceeded with the next phase of her classes.

During her year away from school, being naturally curious, Udoka had decided to sharpen her intellect by reading books of various genres, after work hours. She began with self-help books before graduating to other areas such as race, feminism, business, and so on. The more books she read on Black culture, the more she realized how ignorant she was about the history of racism in America. She read about the transatlantic slave trade, Jim Crow laws, and the civil rights movement. She read about civil rights leaders such as W.E.B. Du Bois, who was a founding member of the National Association for the Advancement of Colored People (NAACP); Thurgood Marshall, who was the first Black supreme court justice; Rosa Parks, who was known for her significant role in the Montgomery bus boycott; Martin Luther King Jr., who was known for promoting non-violent resistance; among others. Malcolm X's autobiography specifically shifted something in her. She was mesmerized by his radicalism. She respected Martin Luther King Jr.'s views on peaceful activism but identified more with Malcolm X's views on using violence when necessary. With each chapter of his autobiography she read, there was increased anger rising within her. She wanted to continue his fight against racism. Why didn't American colleges have mandatory classes on the history of the civil rights movement? Was the U.S. education system deliberately trying to bury its racist past? Udoka was happy to learn about the Black Lives Matter movement, and the works of Ava DuVernay such as the "13th" documentary and "When They See Us" drama miniseries which highlighted modern day issues on racism. From "13th," Udoka learned about the 13th amendment in the U.S. constitution which explained that although slavery was abolished, a person could still be used for free labor if found to be a felon. Hence, although Blacks were freed from slavery, racist administrations made strategic efforts to criminalize the Black man, leading to mass incarceration, thus modern slavery. Udoka read articles that addressed controversies about the CIA being involved in introducing crack cocaine into Black neighborhoods in the 1980s. As addictions rose, instead of the U.S. government declaring a health epidemic, it criminalized crack cocaine users who happened to be mostly Black. Why then did the same government refuse to criminalize Whites whom the opioids crisis affected the most?

By the time Udoka returned to school to begin her junior year, she was a changed person. To learn more about Black culture in America, she signed up for as many African American studies electives that her degree program could permit. She found the "History of Hip-Hop" class to be the most fascinating. Before taking the class, she had initially viewed hip-hop, mainly rap, as a genre of music that commonly encouraged violence, misogyny, and the use of harmful drugs within Black communities. Surprisingly, while taking the class, she began to learn that early hip-hop music had been used primarily as a medium for social activism but had gradually become mainstream and superficial as time had gone by. Her favorite controversial hip-hop group from the 1980s was Public Enemy. They were the most influential group in their time because of their guts in sending out radical political messages through their music.

With each new day, Udoka became more passionate about Black culture and angrier about the ongoing racism in America. She became more sensitive toward microaggressions and was quick to call out friends and acquaintances on their ignorance. She frequently found herself gravitating towards student activists on campus. The first student activists who caught her attention happened to be two African American third-year students. They had started a campaign to take down the Confederate flag which was still being flown on the school campus. Udoka, wondering what the fuss over a simple flag was about, was eager to find out about the activists' campaign. She soon learned that the Confederate flag was a common White supremacist symbol still being flown by white supremacist organizations such as the Ku Klux Klan (KKK). Udoka was startled. Why was her school still flying a racist flag on campus? Was her school administration racist? Udoka was confused. How could a school which bragged about inclusion decide to keep flying a flag which clearly stood for White supremacy? Still processing the controversy surrounding the flag, Udoka was devastated again to find out that there was a Confederate statue erected in the middle of campus. Before then, Udoka had passed by the statue multiple times, but never really bothered to find out its meaning. She was furious. Investigating why the activists were not protesting the statue as well, she eventually learned that the state of Mississippi, which had a deeply racist administration, was funding major academic programs on the school campus. As a result of the activists' campaign, the administration had already begun threatening to pull their funding upon the removal of the Confederate flag, thus the activists had to compromise.

Udoka took part in the multiple protests organized by the student activists to take down the flag. She helped to design political banners for protest marches around the school campus. To Udoka's surprise, the volunteer marchers turned out to be students and staff of all races and ethnicities. She had expected the marchers to be primarily Black students, but she was proven wrong. Although Mississippi University still had a lot to improve on regarding inclusion, a large percentage of its members were clearly socially aware enough to protest injustices on campus. The protests began peacefully until some members of the KKK suddenly showed up on campus one afternoon. A fight broke out between the Klan and the marchers, and five students were injured. The KKK quickly fled the scene before the police could intervene. Although some marchers had taken videos of the brawl, the cops were unable to track down the perpetrators because they had worn their usual white hoods which hid their faces. The injured students were taken into ambulances while the protest was postponed until better security measures were incorporated to protect future marchers from physical harm.

After weeks of tireless protests, the flag was eventually taken down. The event made the national news, and the student leaders of the campaign were celebrated locally and nationally. Udoka, inspired by them, began to read up on their profiles, with the hope of emulating their lifestyles. Upon learning that they were members of a historically Black sorority, Alpha Sigma Theta (AST), she began to consider joining the sorority. The day she made her final decision to join was the day she realized that the sorority was founded by ten African American women who were prominent figures in the civil rights movement. The sorority was founded on public service and sisterhood. Udoka, being passionate about African American culture and activism, knew right away that AST was made for her. She longed to be part of the sisterhood which bred a community of changemakers. Udoka spent a year preparing to pledge the sorority. She attended their events frequently and connected with their members. Once the application season began, Udoka was instructed to turn in recommendation letters from active AST members who could attest to her involvement in public service. Thus, she sought assistance from the student activists whom she had worked with the previous year to take down the Confederate flag. Impressed with her contribution towards their campaign, they were overjoyed to write her recommendation letters.

Udoka was excited to have been accepted to pledge into the sorority. Once the pledging season began, she opted to take fewer classes than usual to make time to attend the mandatory pledging functions. Black sororities and fraternities had a rule that no intake was allowed to discuss their pledging process with anyone during or after the process; hence, Udoka refrained from informing her friends and family. Being "on line" was typically agonizing for intakes. The process involved subjecting the intakes to rigorous mental and physical tasks to test their dedication towards joining the sorority. Udoka's pledging process lasted a month while she persevered through each day's excruciating tasks. On her line, she was the only African among African American intakes, and thus had to put in extra effort to be accepted socially. A few intakes were snobbish towards her initially, but eventually warmed up to her as they bonded over team activities. Later, when she asked them why they had been harsh at first, they explained that they disliked Africans in America for habitually bragging about being better than African Americans. Udoka was disappointed that Africans in America could be arrogant enough to insult the people whose ancestors fought for civil rights—an aftermath which they were benefiting from. After Udoka successfully completed the pledging process, she decided to inform her parents of her involvement in her new sorority. One late afternoon, she did a video call with her father in Nigeria and her mother in Houston, Texas. Instead of congratulating her, to her dismay, her parents screamed, insisting that she had abandoned her studies and joined a cult. Udoka laughed out loud before explaining to them that sororities in American colleges were completely different from cults in Nigerian universities. American Black sororities were focused on uplifting their members morally and academically, while cults in Nigerian schools were dangerous organizations that promoted crime on campus. After thirty minutes of persuasion, her parents finally accepted her decision.

AST sorority was popular on campus for organizing innovative and vibrant social and public service events during AST week, which took place once a semester. Each Black sorority was assigned a week every semester to organize events pertaining to values they upheld within their organizations. The events were typically open to the public. To contribute towards the upcoming AST week, Udoka decided to tap into her Nigerian culture and her knowledge of neuroscience and psychology. She volunteered to organize AST's International Awareness Day. She partnered with ACSA to perform a traditional dance that showcased African and Afro-Caribbean culture at the event. She prepared popular African dishes for the attendees and sought help from the Afro-Caribbean ACSA members to prepare their native dishes. She showcased PowerPoint slides that discussed fun facts about African and Afro-Caribbean culture, and debunked stereotypes about the two cultures. She ended the event by playing a popular Afro-Caribbean song, "Follow the Leader," by The Soca Boys, and led the attendees to dance around the auditorium in a single line. Udoka's International Awareness Day event was a huge success. After that day, numerous African American students became interested in learning more about African and Afro-Caribbean culture, and thus started attending ACSA events regularly. ACSA in return, began partnering with Black-affiliated organizations on campus such as NAACP and Black Student Union, during Black history month, to organize events that celebrated the diversity of Black culture. Udoka was proud of her involvement in fostering unity among Black students on campus.

    To further contribute towards her first AST week, for Mental Health Day, Udoka being a neuroscience and psychology major, partnered with a dyslexia-focused non-profit organization to administer dyslexia screening tests on campus. Following up on the results of the dyslexia screening, Udoka encouraged the newly aware dyslexic students to take advantage of the university's accommodations for learning disabilities. She also invited a few Black therapists to campus to discuss common psychological issues predominant among Blacks, and the need for mental health awareness within the Black community. With the assistance of the Black therapists whom she invited, she successfully connected numerous Black students on campus to Black therapists across the country. She encouraged the students to try virtual therapy sessions which would expose them to a wider range of Black therapists within and outside of their immediate communities.

The therapists whom Udoka invited, during their sessions on campus, also discussed understanding phobias and anxieties. They introduced students to past life regression therapy which had been proven to help people decipher the roots of their phobias and anxieties. The therapists described past life regression therapy to be a method that used hypnosis to retrieve memories of past lives and incarnations. They then performed past life regressions on some curious Black students and found some of their phobias to be rooted in years of slavery. The therapists suspected that many African Americans were probably repressed from the trauma of being slaves in their past lives. Udoka, curious about her own phobias, asked the therapists to conduct a session for her. She was eager to understand an occurrence from her freshman year. During that year, for every new part-time maid job she got, she would faint on the first day at the job. Unfortunately, the fainting would continue every time she showed up for work. Sadly, she was eventually fired from five different maid jobs for being unfit to work. Udoka could never understand why her body would always fail her at every new maid job. In the end, she quit trying to be a part-time maid and found a job on campus as a part-time bookstore cashier. Interestingly, she never fainted during her time as a cashier. Empathizing with Udoka, one of the therapists then performed a past life regression on her and found out that she had been a maltreated maid in her previous life. In this old life, Udoka had fainted multiple times from being beaten badly by her employer who eventually beat her to death one day. She had clearly carried this trauma from her old life into her new life, thus explaining why she would always faint at every new job as a maid. Udoka was astonished. The therapists then advised her to undergo therapy in the future to heal from the trauma.

Before leaving, the therapists also taught students how to read their Akashic records by themselves. They referred to the Akashic records as the Book of Life which contained the past, present, and future of all universal events. They mentioned that one could typically access the Akashic records through the Pathway Prayer said in a silent room, with a centered mind. They then distributed copies of the Pathway Prayer to students:

OPENING PRAYER

And so we do acknowledge the Forces of Light

Asking for guidance, direction, and courage to know the

Truth as it is revealed for our highest good and the

highest good of everyone connected to us.

Oh Holy Spirit of God,

Protect me from all forms of self-centeredness

And direct my attention to the work at hand.

Help me to know (*myself/first name of individual being read*)

in the light of the Akashic Records,

To see (*myself/first name of individual being read*)

through the eyes of the Lords of the Records,

And enable me to share the wisdom and compassion that the Masters, Teachers, and Loved Ones

of (*me/first name of individual being read*) have for (*me/them*).

*Repeat this second section 1x out loud and 2x silently to self.

The Records are now open.

CLOSING PRAYER

I would like to thank the Masters, Teachers, and Loved Ones

for their love and compassion.

I would like to thank the Lords of the Akashic Records

for their point of view.

And I would like to thank the Holy Spirit of Light for all knowledge and healing.

The Records are now closed. Amen

The Records are now closed. Amen

The Records are now closed. Amen

The therapists mentioned that once opened, information from the Akashic records would then be presented to each person in unique forms e.g., through a trance, angel numbers, etc. Also, Lords of the Records, who were non-physical Light Beings, guarded the Akashic Records and were selective about information they presented to inquirers. They only gave information which they knew would help the seekers ascend through their spiritual path. No person, without permission, was allowed to inquire about another person's Akashic records.

Chapter 5

Aina, having left Nigeria at a young age to pursue better education, had never returned until the launch of her television show. After living in the diaspora for so long, she was excited that her show, Tiger's Den, would be a chance for her to finally contribute towards Africa development. Tiger's Den would play a huge role in presenting Africa to the world, as a continent filled with talent and business opportunities. Aina was exhausted with the typical media portrayal of Africa as a poverty-stricken continent. While working as an investor for Nigerian businesses, she enjoyed meeting young entrepreneurs and spotlighting their growing businesses through her show. The success of Tiger's Den made Aina become more eager to deepen her ties with the country. She began to brainstorm additional ways to spotlight Nigeria's rich culture.

One afternoon, during one of their lengthy catch-up sessions, Udoka informed Aina about how much she was learning about Black culture through books. Inspired by her friend's inquisitiveness, Aina too wanted to explore Black culture, specifically the history of African culture. Unlike Udoka, Aina struggled with intense reading because of her dyslexia. As a result, she decided to rely on audiobooks and documentaries to learn about African culture, especially those on Nigerian heritage. She learned about political historical figures; the 1967 civil war; the colonization era; the pursuit of independence; the evolution of fashion, music, and religion; and so on. She took a keen interest in Fela Kuti, Africa's musical genius, who through his music, highlighted controversial issues affecting Nigerians. He pioneered Afrobeat and was notorious for using his lyrics to question the Nigerian government. Aina was inspired by his valor in telling stories of his culture through his art. She wanted to emulate him but knew that she was not gifted in music. Could she possibly channel Fela's technique through fashion?

Aina eventually decided to explore telling stories of Nigerian culture and its social issues through clothing patterns. For example, being from a Yoruba home, she thought about depicting Yoruba culture via textile patterns that came in the form of mosaic; pointillism; abstract art such as cubism, expressionism, surrealism; and other creative print designs. To insert the patterns onto fabric, she thought about using techniques such as screen printing; sewing motifs onto fabric using colorful thread; embedding wax prints onto fabric; sewing patterns made from a different fabric onto another fabric; using starch to paint patterns onto a fabric before insertion into dye; and using rhinestones and pearls to create patterns on fabric.

She planned to portray aspects of Yoruba culture such as Egungun masquerade ceremonies, Yoruba naming ceremonies, Yoruba wedding ceremonies, Yoruba market scenes, and so on. If this idea was successful, she would branch out into other tribal cultures within Nigeria. Using the same idea, she also targeted highlighting pressing social issues within Nigeria. She wanted to tell stories on social injustices in Nigeria via textile patterns. For example, she could portray a child's clitoris being cut to depict female genital mutilation; a schizophrenic person being burned alive to illustrate the urgent need for mental health awareness and institutions; a long line of patients waiting to see a doctor to represent the low doctor-to-patient ratio; policemen beating up citizens to portray police brutality; a woman ironing her maids breasts to depict the maltreatment of maids; a widow being thrown out of her home to illustrate the maltreatment of widows; a pregnant woman with leaking feces and urine to depict obstetric fistula; a man beating up his wife and kids to portray domestic violence; women with no breasts to signify the breast cancer epidemic; and other numerous ongoing social issues in Nigeria. Aina's long term plan for this fashion idea was to make it mainstream such that Nigerians would normalize wearing artistic clothes that depicted social problems happening in their communities. This strategy had the capacity to force Nigerians to keep having conversations surrounding ways to combat the social problems that were being brought to light everyday via clothing designs. To implement this idea, she launched a clothing brand in Nigeria called "Fun Wa" which meant "For Us" in Yoruba.

Aina hired the most creative fine artists and textile design experts she could find across Nigeria to begin designing the patterns, which would later be transferred onto durable fabrics. Among these fabrics were handmade textiles woven by Nigerian weavers. Aina planned to create more job opportunities for Nigerian youth by hiring weavers in place of machines. She then hired tailors to sew the imprinted fabrics into stylish wearable t-shirts, skirts, dresses, trousers, bags, socks etc. Like her Oyatosi clothing brand, Aina also transferred the textile patterns onto interior design items such as wallpapers, carpets, pillowcases, couch covers, bedsheets, etc. which she later sold in retail stores. To launch her Fun Wa clothing brand, first, she applied to showcase her line at the Lagos Fashion Week. Next, she publicized the brand further via social media and television stations. Orders started to pour in, especially from Nigerians who already knew her as the founder of Oyatosi and Tiger's Den. Activists wanted to wear her clothes for their campaigns. Artistes wanted to wear her clothes for their music videos. Lay Nigerians wanted to wear her clothes to school, work, parties, and everywhere else.

For her first fashion show at the Lagos Fashion Week, Aina chose to include political and cultural hairstyles to accentuate her Fun Wa clothing brand showcase. To prepare for the show, she sought hairstylists who were skilled in making cultural and political hairstyles. She eventually came across Laetitia Ky's work on Instagram. Laetitia Ky was a feminist artist from Ivory Coast who created sculptures from her hair. Some of her hair sculptures with feminist political messages included: a man lifting a woman's skirt inappropriately; a man's hand drugging a woman's drink; the female reproductive system; and many more. She also designed apolitical hair sculptures such as the shape of Africa, an umbrella, a snowman, a broken heart, a bulb, among others. Ibilola was astonished by Laetitia's work. She had never seen this form of art in her entire life. She immediately contacted Laetitia to propose hiring her as a hairstylist for her fashion show. Laetitia agreed to the job offer and was flown to Lagos in time for the Lagos Fashion Week. Laetitia ensured that all Aina's models got faux locs at least a week before the fashion show; she knew that she would be turning their faux locs into tight, slightly heavy hair sculptures, and thus wanted them to have at least a full week for their scalps to heal from installing their new locs. The fashion show turned out successful, and Laetitia agreed to Aina's job offer to be the primary hairstylist for her subsequent fashion shows.

Aina's competitive advantage was the uniqueness in her ability to tell important stories of her people via clothing patterns. She emerged successful in portraying Yoruba culture, and thus began to expand into other cultures across Nigeria. In interviews about her clothing brand, she attributed the success of Fun Wa brand to being inspired by Fela Kuti's music. To make her next fashion shows more memorable, she added dramatic performances that depicted the social issues which were being illustrated on the clothes being showcased. For example, if the first line of clothes to be showcased was to highlight mental health awareness, she would begin the show with a mime theatrical performance that told a story on mental health awareness. Aina developed this idea after watching documentaries on British fashion designer, Alexander McQueen, who was popular for his edgy and political fashion show theatrics.

The more Aina learned about Alexander McQueen, the more motivated she was to get in touch with her dark side. She began fantasizing about creating fashion that depicted dangerously political views. Once, she thought about designing patterns that portrayed the assassination of corrupt Nigerian politicians. Another day, she contemplated creating designs that showcased a group of women hanging a notorious rapist to death. Next, she foresaw producing designs that represented Nigerians burning members of a dangerous cult alive. She envisioned bringing thriller into her fashion brand with a goal to send warning messages to immoral Nigerians. Contrary to advice from friends and family, Aina went ahead to launch this new controversial fashion line.

One week after her clothing line was launched, Aina was kidnapped by military men on her way out of her house to a late-night event. The governor of Lagos State, Bola Adeyemi, had instructed the men to hold her hostage in a jail cell for two weeks until his political campaign was over. He was running for the second term of the Lagos State governor's office and was determined to get rid of any threat to his campaign. A week prior to her arrest, Aina had released a clothing line that portrayed the assassination of corrupt Nigerian politicians, and Governor Adeyemi happened to be one of the politicians depicted. Governor Adeyemi was a dangerous politician who was rumored to be a member of one of the most notorious cultist gangs in Lagos. He was suspected to be behind the assassinations of numerous politicians who were courageous enough to expose some of his ill-doings. As public as some of his criminal escapades were, he never seemed to be convicted because of his connections with the Lagos State judiciary. A percentage of the money he embezzled from Lagos State funds typically went to his allies within the judiciary, in exchange for his protection from being prosecuted. For every court trial Governor Adeyemi underwent, he always seemed to be acquitted, and as long as he maintained an innocent public image, he still had public supporters. Many Nigerians knew he was a corrupt politician, but others refused to rely on hearsay. They were bent on denouncing him only if the court of law condemned him as a criminal. Until then, he remained innocent in their eyes.

At the station, before being thrown into a jail cell, Aina was first beaten by the jail guards and then asked to strip off. She handed over her Calvin Klein black dress, Christian Louboutin heels, and gold jewelry, but was allowed to remain in her underwear. After seizing her clothes, the guards stared at her half naked body like tigers contemplating whether to pounce on a potential prey. Aina knew there was a possibility of her being raped that night. Drenched in tears, she squatted to hide her nakedness while nursing her bruises. Fortunately for her, to a typical Nigerian man, she was not regarded as a mainstream pretty girl. Beauty standards in the country favored mostly light-skinned, curvy, and petite women. Aina was the opposite. She was dark-skinned, six feet, and as straight as a ruler. This night was the first time Aina was grateful for having a "non-attractive" physique which kept her from being raped. After analyzing her physique, the guards hissed and mumbled insults about her looks while walking away. Aina was relieved but was also still in a lot of pain from her fresh bruises.

The jail cell smelled so much of stale urine and dead rats that Aina had to throw up in a corner. She wondered where she would sleep that night. The floor was too dirty for her to let the rest of her skin touch it. She was already worried about having an infection on her soles which had touched the floor. Aina squatted for hours with her back against the wall, wondering what her fate was going to be. After four hours of squatting with trembling knees, and doing jumping jacks in-between to avoid spasms, she knew she had to do something about her situation. She stood up and called to one of the guards to bring her a cup of water, insisting that she was on the verge of dying from thirst. "Only because you be American celebrity. Oga say make we keep you alive, make U.S. government no come arrest us upon your dead body," mumbled the guard. This statement was what assured Aina that she was not going to be killed in the cell. It explained why such a dangerous politician, suspected to have murdered his opponents in the past, had speared her life. He was probably worried that as a celebrity in America, her death would attract international scrutiny and consequences, which he did not have the power to fight or hide from. Aina was given the cup of water which she splashed on a small section of the floor to shift the dirt to a different corner. Satisfied with the much cleaner-looking floor section, she was willing to risk sitting on the floor with her bare butt.

Meanwhile, her new controversial clothing line had become the most popular topic among Nigerians. Religious Nigerians shamed her for fostering hate within the country. Other Nigerians praised her for her audacity. Politicians called her out for putting their lives in danger. The media had gone haywire over Aina's new line.

Interview requests poured in from the press, but nobody knew where Aina was. Her driver and gateman had been killed during the kidnapping. While in Lagos, Aina had lived alone. Her parents had relocated to Ondo State, their hometown, some years after she had moved to the U.S. to live as an adopted child of her aunt. Back in the jail cell, the military men had seized her phone; hence, she had no way to contact anyone. After two days of Aina being missing, her friends began searching for her. They went to her house, but it was locked. They banged on the gate for an hour, but no one responded. There were no traces of the kidnapping because Governor Adeyemi had instructed some of his men to get rid of the dead bodies of the driver and the gateman. They were also instructed to park Aina's car into her compound, clean it up to get rid of the blood of the driver, and then lock her gate. There were no bystanders when the kidnapping happened because Aina's house was inside a high-end estate which was secluded from public spaces. The estate was known to be one of the safest in Lagos where celebrities resided, but Governor Adeyemi, being well-connected, was easily able to track down Aina's whereabouts.

On her second day of being held hostage, Aina knew she could not survive a week in the cell. Her body was still sore from bruises; she was hungry and thirsty; and she needed to lie down after sleeping through two nights in a sitting position. She had to come up with a plan, but she was too weak to think clearly. She waited to be served breakfast. When the guard placed her breakfast tray in her cell, she nearly threw up. The bread she was served had mold, while the yogurt had separated into two layers, with a spider web floating on the top. Aina asked the guard to take the food away. The trauma from her breakfast encounter made Aina garner enough strength to come up with an urgent escape plan.

She feigned being epileptic, pleading with the guard to take her to a clinic to get her medication in case of a seizure. She explained that her body, being under extreme stress, could trigger a seizure. Her body had been badly injured; her heart rate was high from extreme anxiety; and she had not eaten in two days. The guard seemed concerned at first but ignored her. Aina gave him about thirty minutes to change his mind before faking an epileptic seizure. Panicking and not having enough time to think through his actions, the guard quickly called an ambulance. He took off his inner shirt and put it on the half-naked Aina before she was placed on the stretcher. By then, his partner had pawned her expensive dress and other belongings.

An hour after Aina was dropped off at the hospital, the entrance became swarmed with press eager to interview her. The guard who had accompanied her, upon seeing the press outside, knew right away that he had failed in his duties to Governor Adeyemi. The governor had wanted Aina out of sight for two weeks until his election campaign was over. As the guard was weighing the consequences of his action, his partner rushed through the hospital doors furious. "Oba, wetin you do?! Where Aina dey?! Wetin you do?!" He was pacing back and forth, panting profusely. "Governor don vex finish! Im say you be dead man. Im don vex for me sote I come run from im office. Oba, wetin you do?!" Oba was in tears. He knew what his fate was about to be. "No be Oga say make we keep am alive?! No be im say im no want trouble with United States?! Na so Aina come get epilepsy for morning. I come catch fear. Na why I call ambulance say make im no die for my hand. Wetin you want make I do?! Oga say make Aina no die, that na why I call ambulance to carry am to hospital! Ye! I don die! Ade, my brother! I don die! Help me abeg!" Oba was on the floor at this point, with his hands on his chest. He was struggling to catch his breath and was clearly having a panic attack. His partner rushed to find a nurse who would give him an oxygen mask. As Oba breathed in and out into the oxygen mask, Ade gave him instructions on how to escape the governor's wrath. He gave him the address of his brother who lived in Ogun State. Oba was instructed to get on the next bus to Ogun State if he was to escape being punished or killed by the governor.

    That afternoon, after Aina was discharged from the hospital, she stopped by the entrance to give a speech to the press still cramped outside. She gave a detailed encounter of her kidnapping and the murder of her driver and gateman. She informed the press that if she were ever to go missing again, Governor Adeyemi should be investigated first, and the United States should be informed that one of their citizens was being held hostage by him. Her parents, friends, and co-workers, upon seeing her speech on the news, immediately rushed to the hospital. Her parents ended up taking her home, accompanied by a military officer whom they had brought with them from Ondo State. That week, Aina's parents installed stronger security measures in her home, including two trained guard dogs. The governor, upon hearing Aina's speech, knew that he had to keep his distance from her. Still bent on avoiding international scrutiny, he decided not to push back on her controversial statements about him. Within two months of recovering from her bruises and trauma, Aina released another controversial fashion line, showcasing clothes that depicted Governor Adeyemi as a murderer. He was furious but kept his distance. He knew Aina had the upper hand; however, he doubted that her political stunts would last long. He was wrong.

Chapter 6

It was nearing the end of Udoka's junior year, and she knew it was time to turn in her proposals for her psychology and neuroscience final year capstone projects. For neuroscience, she decided she wanted to do research on developmental disorders in children living in low-income areas in America. Udoka picked this topic because of her experience as a former intern, researching childhood development disorders at a neuroscience firm. Upon concluding the internship, she knew instantly that she wanted to pursue this field long-term. She was curious about how involved the government was in providing funding for special needs education. She was also curious about whether these special needs children were exposed to the right amount of emotional support within and outside of school. Udoka had watched a documentary called "Life, Animated," which shed light on how an autistic child relied on watching only cartoons at home to help him understand the way the world worked. His parents, who were heavily involved in meeting his unique needs, indulged him with kid-friendly cartoons, upon learning that his vocabulary and awareness of the world grew mostly from watching cartoons. She had also watched another documentary that detailed the important roles that service and therapy animals, such as dogs, cats, and guinea pigs, played in the lives of special needs kids. Udoka, after watching these documentaries, suddenly became interested in highlighting through her capstone research project, underlying factors hindering the provision of adequate, specialized support within and outside school, to special needs children in low-income communities in America.

Udoka, eager for feedback, spoke with Aina about her plan for her neuroscience capstone project. Aina loved the idea and offered to introduce her to Jessica, an acquaintance who was a philanthropist in the field of childhood developmental disorders. Jessica was a controversial reality television star in Nigeria, who had taken on an atypical approach towards philanthropy, by marrying several husbands with whom she adopted and raised special needs kids. She had chosen to air this aspect of her life on a television show with the intent to promote freedom of sexuality, while also exposing the obstacles with raising special needs children in Nigeria. She wanted to humanize these children as equally important members of the society. She also intended to use a major percentage of the proceeds from the show to provide financial support for the kids.

Udoka, interested in meeting this daring, radical woman, accepted Aina's proposal to connect them. Udoka was interested in connecting with Jessica because she foresaw herself moving back to Nigeria in the future and continuing in the childhood developmental disorders field. It seemed like a smart idea to start early to build her network in the field. Upon meeting Jessica via a video call, their chemistry assured her that they would become long-term friends. They both had overlapping interests in various things, but Udoka was mostly curious about Jessica's background and how it influenced her to launch such a controversial television show.

Jessica began her story by highlighting the end of her second year in college in America, when she had gotten pregnant by her boyfriend. She had wanted to keep the baby, but her boyfriend was not ready to be a father. Jessica decided to raise the child on her own. She dropped out of school which by her first year, already seemed to be a waste of her time. She was bored out of her mind. The only reason she remained in school for two years was to please her parents. Her pregnancy, to her, was a way out of the boring college life. Jessica moved into her parents' mansion until she could figure out how to attain financial independence. Her parents were willing to assist her financially and emotionally, while she figured out her life. They encouraged her to explore entrepreneurship, promising to invest in the most lucrative business idea she could come up with. While contemplating her future financially, Jessica also thought about how she wanted to proceed with her personal life. Would she enjoy being a single mother the rest of her life? Did she want to raise her child in America or Nigeria?

Jessica was born to Nigerian Igbo parents and raised in America. Growing up in America, Jessica's parents had exposed her to Nigerian culture whenever they could. At home, they ate mostly Nigerian dishes and spoke only Igbo; they made her attend multiple Nigerian events hosted in America; they made her watch numerous Nollywood movies, especially ones where Igbo was spoken; and whenever they could, they visited Nigeria during holidays; hence, Jessica grew to love Nigerian culture while also imbibing American culture. However, she still longed to experience living in Nigeria as an independent adult. Overall, Jessica knew that an adventurous, unconventional life would always be her number one priority. She hated following the status quo. She adored Kim Kardashian for being a trailblazer in reality television while simultaneously pursuing a law career to fight for social justice for underrepresented populations. Jessica proceeded with planning her future by first writing out her main interests:

1) Move to Nigeria to raise children
2) Have an unorthodox romantic life
3) Give back to Nigeria via supporting a social cause in the country
4) Start a career in media

    She began brainstorming how to design her future based on the interests she had written out. After a week of introspection, she finally came up with a daring life path. She decided that she would move back to Nigeria with her baby and marry six men who would all live with her in one big compound. Her parents were mortified. She fancied the idea of polyandry which was not common in Nigeria. As a feminist, she wanted to challenge Nigerians to embrace polyandry the same way they had normalized polygyny. If it was acceptable for Nigerian men to marry numerous wives, why then was it abnormal for women to marry numerous husbands? Within her marriage, she planned to pursue philanthropy by adopting a special needs child with each husband. The first child would have Down's syndrome; the second child would be autistic; the third child would be dyslexic; the fourth child would be physically disabled; the fifth child would be blind, and the sixth child would be deaf. Jessica planned to launch a reality television show called "Atypical Family" which would let viewers journey with her as she navigated raising special needs, underrepresented kids with her six husbands. Via a TED talk, "I got 99 problems…palsy is just one" given by Maysoon Zayid, she had learned that people with disabilities were the largest minority in the world and the most underrepresented in entertainment. Jessica wanted to be a leader in creating more positive images of disability in the media and everyday life. Her overall goal was to push boundaries in Nigeria on marriage and philanthropy, and through her television show, expose the inadequate support Nigeria provided for special needs children.

With some investment from her wealthy parents, Jessica bought an expansive plot of land in Banana Island, Lagos. On this land, she built seven beautiful condos. She inhabited one of the condos with her biological child, while the remaining six were each to be inhabited by one husband and one adopted child. Next, she began scouting for potential husbands by attending social events in Lagos. The first fifty men she tried to court concluded that she was deranged, upon hearing about her plan for polyandry. Jessica's marriage arrangement seemed implausible in a heavily patriarchal society such as Lagos. However, before quitting, she decided to give her scouting one last creative try. This time, she resolved to go after young, handsome, male, recent university graduates, preying upon their inability to find decent-paying jobs elsewhere. All they had to do was agree to polyandry and raise disabled adopted children with her. They would also sign a contract detailing their responsibilities within the marriage. General details of each contract included:

1) Husband must remain in the marriage for at least twenty seasons of the show.
2) Forty percent of the proceeds from the show will be split as individual salaries for members of the polyandrous family. The remaining sixty percent will go towards the upkeep of the children.
3) Each husband will be allowed to take on any outside job which would not interfere with his marital and parental responsibilities.
4) Jessica will be allowed to terminate the contract of any husband who is not meeting her standards sexually or parentally.
5) Jessica will have sex with each husband at allocated times during the week. However, every Sunday night, Jessica and her husbands will gather at her condo to have sex together.
6) Each husband must be heavily invested in the upbringing of their adopted child. He will be responsible for assisting Jessica with the academic, extra-curricular, and personal aspects of the child's growth.
7) Anyone within the polyandry who engages in infidelity will forfeit their salary for a year as their first strike. If infidelity occurs more than once, the

member will be dismissed from the marriage indefinitely.

The day the reality television show was launched, there was outrage in Lagos. Within a month, "Atypical Family" became the most controversial and top ten most watched reality show on Netflix in Nigeria. It got mixed reviews from viewers: some were warmed by Jessica's adoption of less-privileged kids; some were annoyed that she was making money off less-privileged kids in the name of "reality television;" feminists hailed her for disrupting patriarchy in her marriage; anti-feminists insulted her for emasculating her husbands; some viewers insisted that she was an attention-seeker; religious viewers shamed her for promoting immoral sexuality; and so on. Although Jessica and her husbands were constantly threatened and trolled online, they persisted with the show. By the end of the first season, the uproar had subsided, and "Atypical Family" slowly became a success. Jessica became known nationally for shaping a new culture of sexuality and family life in a notoriously patriarchal country.

Udoka was startled by Jessica's guts. Alongside Aina, Jessica was one of the most fearless women she had ever met. She was grateful to have these two women in her life, inspiring her to push boundaries.

After her interesting conversation with Jessica, Udoka went back to picking a topic for her psychology capstone project. Udoka's proposal centered on researching the prevalence and acceptability of past life regression therapy within Black communities in America to help heal their cycle of trauma.

Once her capstone proposals were approved by her academic advisors, Udoka began her research. Her final year in college was particularly brutal because she had to complete her capstone projects while juggling her usual rigorous class schedule. Although progressing in her capstone research, she struggled in class team projects because she could not learn her class materials in time to contribute towards group projects. Udoka's schedule kept clashing with her team members' schedules, and in no time, they began to report her to the teachers overseeing each course. Knowing that she was typically the only Black student in most of her classes, Udoka felt humiliated every time she was singled out for not contributing enough to team projects. She had spent her college years working extra hard to excel academically with a goal to debunk the stereotype that Black people were unintelligent and lazy. She desperately longed to be in a space where she could excel and fail without worrying about its association with her race.

In one of her classes, there was one other Black student called Alexa, who was biracial. Udoka had hoped that they would support each other, considering that they were the only Black students in their class. Unfortunately, Udoka soon learned that Alexa harbored self-hate. Alexa had always been secretly ashamed of her Black side, but only embodied it when she needed favors from Black people. She only realized she was Black when she needed support from the National Society of Black Psychologists

(NSBS) Mississippi University chapter to sponsor her trip to their annual conference and career fair; she only realized she was Black when she wanted to pledge AST sorority, a historically Black sorority, but was denied because of her low GPA. She desperately wanted validation from her White classmates to the extent of insulting Black people in their presence to prove her allegiance to the White race. In Udoka's eyes, Alexa was an embarrassment to the Black race. Udoka once heard a rumor about her that in her sophomore year, she was on the verge of failing a core class. Desperate to escape the humiliation from her White classmates, she had offered to sleep with the teaching assistant (TA) of that class in exchange for higher grades. The TA, disgusted with her behavior, reported her to the professor who then sent out a mass email, warning her students about the implications of offering sex for grades. Alexa's name was not mentioned in the email, but the rumor about her began after two students in that class had passed by the professor's office and seen her crying and begging for forgiveness.

Throughout the academic year, Udoka kept struggling to catch up in multiple team projects. In projects where she could catch up with her team, they would be skeptical of her contribution, generally assuming that she was not intelligent enough to get right answers. Udoka would solve a portion of the team project, and then present her results to her team. They would then take her work, but in her absence, would recalculate what she had initially solved, usually getting the same answers she had gotten. When team evaluations came along, they would rate Udoka low, insisting that they had solved all the project questions without her help, even though she had contributed to the team, but was never trusted to produce accurate answers. Udoka was devastated because team evaluations typically impacted a huge chunk of students' grades. She complained to the teacher, but he did nothing about the situation. He was an ignorant White man with white fragility who avoided any issues of racism in his class. She reported the situation to the head of department who was unfortunately another ignorant White man.

Udoka was frustrated by her teammates but even more irritated by her professor and the head of department for their phoniness. They were the only professors who had added her as a friend on Facebook and were quick to comment on every new hairstyle she had worn to class; however, they were also the first ones to desert her when she began struggling in her senior year. In Udoka's opinion, they seemed more concerned about appearing likable rather than embodying true compassion. She began to count down desperately to her graduation. Before her senior year, Udoka was used to getting mostly "A" grades and some "B" grades in her classes. However, with the unexpected turn that her senior year had taken, she finally settled with multiple "C" grades in some classes. Her GPA ended up dropping by some points at the end of the academic year but was still high enough for her to graduate with honors. She was nevertheless grateful to have aced her capstone project presentations.

On graduation day, before proceeding to the hall, Udoka sat alone in her room and poured herself a glass of expensive champagne. She then made a toast to herself, celebrating her resilience in pushing through racism in college, while evolving into a well-rounded, gutsy woman. Upon walking across the graduation stage, she made sure to reject the phony hugs and handshakes extended from the head of department and professor who had deserted her in her senior year. She hugged and shook the rest of the professors who had been genuinely supportive. The next day, accompanied by her mother, Udoka packed her belongings and moved out of Mississippi University, vowing never to return except to empower the Black students there. She prayed to be wealthy enough in the future to come back to offer annual scholarship awards to high-achieving Black students at her alma-mater. Following her departure from Mississippi University, Udoka went on to work as a full-time hire at the last neuroscience firm she had interned for. There, she assisted with more advanced research on childhood development disorders.

Chapter 7

Aina continued designing provocative outfits. Her next line centered on celebrating nakedness and debunking beauty standards. She designed outfits that portrayed naked men and women of all sizes. She also incorporated women with hairy armpits, pubic hair, and hairy legs, to start a conversation about ending body hair shaming. In her second year of releasing political clothing lines, a strange thing happened. While shopping at a supermarket, she ran into an individual whom she could not classify as male or female. This strange individual had an ambiguous look that she simply could not label. They began chatting while in line to pay for their groceries, and she soon learned that this individual's name was Tomiwa. Tomiwa could either be a boy or girl's name, she thought to herself. Interested in getting to know each other, they both decided to meet up for lunch that coming weekend. Aina was excited to get to know this strange-looking individual.

During lunch, she learned that Tomiwa was an audio engineer, and was intersex. She had heard the term "intersex" once or twice but had never bothered to inquire about its meaning. Tomiwa explained to her that an intersex individual was someone who embodied both male and female sex characteristics with respect to chromosomes, gonads, sex hormones, or genitals. The person was basically born with a combination of male and female biological traits, and typically had sex organs which were abnormally large or small. Being intersex, Tomiwa had chosen their pronouns to be they/them/theirs. They revealed to Aina about how they had struggled with their identity when they were younger. Tomiwa was born with a vagina, as well as ovotestes which were gonads that had both ovarian and testicular tissue. Although they had a big clitoris, they also had male sex characteristics such as a deep masculine voice with a wide chest that had no breasts. Tomiwa's family concluded that they were a girl, but a tom-boy. As a teenager, Tomiwa was continually teased by their female classmates for being the only girl in their class with no breasts. They were the only girl who was supposedly late to puberty. The girls avoided hanging out with Tomiwa who was seen as too rough and masculine. Tomiwa ended up regularly playing with boys who enjoyed their company platonically, but never romantically. They developed an identity crisis and began searching for why they were so different from other girls. How could they be a girl but also look and sound like a man? Tomiwa's mother, after consulting with multiple physicians, finally found a renowned doctor who explained that Tomiwa was an intersex. Unfortunately, Tomiwa's extended family in their village was not accepting of their condition, citing that they were a product of witchcraft. Some even threatened to kill them if they ever attended family functions. Aina was astounded. Tomiwa, upon reading online about other intersex people's experiences, found that they too experienced early stages of humiliation from their peers. For example, an intersex woman, who was born with ambiguous sex organs, wrote about being raised as a boy until she had her period in class one day. After that day, she was mocked consistently for being a freak.

In the process of searching online for intersex support groups in Nigeria, Tomiwa connected with two intersex persons who eventually became their good friends:

Ebuka, who identified as an intersex man, was raised as a boy when he was young, because he had a penis. But as he grew older, while having a micropenis and a masculine-shaped face, he also developed breasts and feminine curves, and maintained a high-pitched voice. He never menstruated but had monthly pains on the sides of his abdomen which turned out to be ovulation pains. Ebuka was repeatedly bullied in school, beaten up, and called a weirdo by other boys. Traumatized from the bullying, he requested to transfer to a different school. After consulting a doctor to understand his condition, he realized he was intersex. He was informed that as an intersex, although he had a penis, he also had ovaries but no uterus which explained the ovulation pains but no menstruation. Ebuka eventually had surgery to remove his ovaries and began taking testosterone pills to enhance his male sex characteristics.

Sandra identified as an intersex woman. When she was a child, she had a hernia, which was the bulging of an organ or tissue through an abnormal opening. She was immediately taken to the hospital. When the doctors cut her open, they found testes where ovaries should have been. She was then diagnosed with androgen insensitivity syndrome (AIS), meaning that instead of having two X chromosomes like other girls, she had an X and a Y chromosome. Sandra ended up developing outer female characteristics such as the presence of a vagina and breasts, but she had no uterus, fallopian tubes, or a cervix. Thus, as a teenager she was unable to menstruate like other girls in her class. Her Y chromosome had told her body to produce testes. But once her testes began to function normally, producing lots of androgens, Sandra's body did not respond to them. This occurrence was because of her insensitivity to androgens, thus resulting in AIS. Sandra eventually had her testes removed. Sandra, as a young girl, luckily did not go through intense bullying for being intersex because she was able to keep it a secret. She had outer female characteristics; hence, nobody knew she was genetically male unless she told them. Then, the only people who knew about her intersex condition were close family members. Sandra, wanting to maintain her secret, was reluctant to date for a long time. After years of being a single intersex woman, she eventually opened up and found a boyfriend who ended up loving her regardless of her condition. He was even open to adopting kids in the future to start a family with Sandra. Sandra, over time, gradually became open with strangers about her condition. She became a part-time blogger, highlighting her experiences as an intersex woman in Nigeria. She and Tomiwa connected for the first time after Tomiwa stumbled upon her blog while searching for intersex support groups.

Tomiwa introduced Aina to LGBTQIA+ culture. Coming from a conservative and religious home, Aina grew up ignorant about the culture. Her family had raised her to regard homosexuals as sinners. Even her aunt whom she lived with in America reinforced this belief. She was convinced that sex between homosexuals was not natural, insisting that the only type of natural sex was between a man and a woman. When Aina informed Tomiwa of this assumption, they laughed. They then went on to explain that men could have sex with men because the prostate, which was the male G-spot, was in the anal area which had a hole for another man to insert his penis into. Also, women could have sex with women because the clitoris, which provided sexual pleasure, was on the surface of the vaginal area. No penetration was needed. Women could orgasm not just through the stimulation of the G-spot from penetration, but also from clitoral stimulation. Tomiwa, being aware that Nigeria still had a homophobic culture, often sought foreign movies and documentaries that empowered LGBTQIA+ culture. They introduced Aina to the "Paris Is Burning" documentary and "Pose" television series on Netflix. Aina was also introduced to audio books on LGBTQIA+ experiences, and particularly enjoyed the memoirs of Janet Mock, a trans woman, and Billy Porter, her favorite gay actor from the "Pose" television series. She watched more documentaries, mainly enjoying "How to Survive a Plague," which detailed the early years of the AIDS epidemic and how it affected gay communities. She began listening to music by international gay icons and became fond of Lil Nas X, a young, Black, unapologetic, gay, American rapper.

    Aina began to research online about Nigeria's homophobic culture and was devastated to find out that the country was still putting homosexuals in jail for fourteen years. She was furious and determined to fight this inhumane law. She began by designing clothing that celebrated LGBTQIA+ culture. In her designs, she depicted gay men having sex; lesbians having sex; bisexual women and men having sex with both genders; trans culture; intersex individuals embodying male and female sex organs; among others. As soon as her LGBTQIA+ line was launched, sales from her Fun Wa clothing brand went down drastically. Homophobic Nigerians began to boycott her brand. The protests went on continuously for weeks and seemed to be expanding every week. In the past, after launching a new controversial line, Aina would expect short-lived backlash which typically lasted about two weeks, before dying down. However, this time, the resistance seemed unending. Aina began receiving death threats while being called "devil's incarnate" and "daughter of Jezebel," by religious fanatics. Aina, after receiving continuous death threats for more than a month, became increasingly worried about her safety. She installed a stronger security system in her home and hired two bodyguards to accompany her everywhere she went. Homophobic Nigerians, in addition to boycotting her brand, began to campaign for her to be dismissed from the country. They insisted that she was using her influence to promote homosexuality which was a grave crime in the country.

  Governor Adeyemi was elated by the public's campaigns to ban Aina from Nigeria. He had finally found a reason to cancel her. First, he proceeded to ban Aina from Lagos State indefinitely. Next, he endorsed and funded the campaigns to ban her from the country, calling on the president to have the final say. In the meantime, following her ban from Lagos, Aina moved to Ondo state to live with her parents, temporarily shutting down her

Lagos fashion office. Her friends and family advised her to move back to the U.S., but she rejected the idea, insisting that her fight was not over. She was certain that part of her life purpose was to be a changemaker in Nigeria. Aina recounted stories of Fela Kuti's turbulent experience with the Nigerian government, citing its similarities with her own experience. She proposed the possibility that she could be a reincarnation of Fela. Her people were astonished. They finally agreed that they were looking at a female version of Fela Kuti. From then onwards, her friends and family nicknamed her "Fela Obinrin," meaning "female Fela" in Yoruba.

After two months of living in Ondo state, the president of Nigeria had still not banned Aina from the country, although Governor Adeyemi was still fueling campaigns for her dismissal. Her case was all over the Nigerian news. Aina refused to give up. Deep down, she knew there was still hope for her to return to Lagos; this situation was simply a test of her perseverance. She held on to Franklin D. Roosevelt's words, "When you reach the end of your rope, tie a knot in it and hang on."

One morning, while having breakfast, she turned on the news and froze in dismay. The president of Nigeria's son, and only child, Gabriel Aminu, had just come out as gay. He was being interviewed on Silverbird Television news. Aina could not believe her eyes. This surprise explained the president's months of silence on her issue. Gabriel explained that he had given his father an ultimatum to either enforce liberty for Aina or watch him leave the country indefinitely. He was calling on Nigerians to protest for the law that criminalized homosexuals to be overturned. Gabriel's interview opened doors for more bombshells throughout the rest of the week. More politicians' kids came out as gay. The Osun state governor's daughter even announced that she was in the process of transitioning into a man. She stated that every time she had traveled on vacation to the United States, she had secretly brought back pills to boost her testosterone hormonal level. She had also planned to schedule a gender reassignment surgery during her next visit. She mentioned that her parents, seeing her suddenly grow facial hair, accompanied with a deepening voice, knew that she was transitioning, but were in denial. They worried in silence about her fate in a homophobic and transphobic Nigeria.

By the end of the week, numerous Nigerians had come out as lesbian, gay, bisexual, intersex, and transitioning; however, the announcement that made Aina laugh out loud the most was that of Governor Adeyemi's daughter who came out as bisexual. In response, the governor was trolled on social media for banning Aina for promoting LGBTQIA+ rights, while his daughter was secretly bisexual. Progressive Nigerians immediately launched campaigns for the governor to overturn Aina's ban. More Nigerians, led by politicians' kids, began a movement across the country to decriminalize LGBTQIA+ rights. The movement garnered international support from progressive countries who threatened to withdraw from trading with Nigeria if it refused to grant liberty to its LGBTQIA+ citizens. In response, after a month of protests, the Supreme Court of Nigeria released a statement that it had successfully overturned the law that criminalized LGBTQIA+ rights. Homosexuals who had been jailed for their sexuality were immediately released. Riots broke out between conservative and progressive Nigerians. There was civil unrest for weeks until the president sent out an army to mitigate the fights. The fights subsided once he released an order for the arrest of anyone who engaged in violent protests.

Meanwhile, Aina had moved back to Lagos and reopened her fashion office. She reunited with Tomiwa, her intersex friend. The more time Aina and Tomiwa spent together, the fonder they became of each other. They both bonded over being outliers in their communities—Aina was dyslexic, while Tomiwa was intersex. Their fondness grew into romance, and in no time, they began dating. Knowing that her love story with Tomiwa was atypical, Aina proposed releasing a book with her non-binary partner in the future, detailing the adventures of dating an intersex in a conservative country. She wanted to challenge the minds of ignorant and judgmental Nigerians through her love story. She also considered launching a reality television show to celebrate their unorthodox relationship.

Although happy in her relationship with Tomiwa, Aina's mental health was deteriorating. She was still being ridiculed by conservative, religious Nigerians for her stance on LGBTQIA+ rights. Thankfully, her Catholic parents, who although were against her views, still accepted her as their daughter. Aina was grateful to have parents who loved her unconditionally, regardless of her political views. With the growing hatred she was receiving from Nigerian Christians, Aina was taken aback by the hypocrisy in the religion. If Christianity supposedly taught unconditional love, why then was she being mocked by mostly Christians for simply promoting sexual and romantic freedom? Why were homosexuals not being seen as deserving of unconditional love? Aina was disappointed. Her skepticism with Christianity also came at a time when she was beginning to consider engaging in sexual relations with Tomiwa. Being raised Christian, she had been taught all her life that sex before marriage was a sin. Aina was conflicted. Was she willing to wait till marriage to explore sexual intimacy with Tomiwa?

With Tomiwa being Aina's first romantic partner, Aina was still naive about how to navigate intimacy in a relationship, especially one with an intersex. To embark on this journey, Aina searched for podcasts and interviews on the romantic and sex lives of intersex people. She found a few, but unfortunately, none of them were comprehensive. "Intersex" was still an avoided topic. Still curious about the adventures of intimacy in a relationship, Aina relied on the podcasts of normal couples who were willing to share insights on the highs and lows within their relationships. She stumbled upon a couple who was struggling to keep their marriage together. They discussed how they had waited till marriage to have sex only to find out that they were sexually incompatible. The woman complained that her husband's huge penis made sex painful for her. The man complained that he was tired of always having to use a lubricant because his wife's vulva was never wet enough during sex. The woman complained that her husband's profuse sweating during sex was disgusting. The man complained that his wife was not seductive enough in the bedroom. He longed for some roleplay which she found to be childish. The woman complained that her husband was too heavy on her during sex and could possibly suffocate her. The man complained that his wife could not "give head" properly and always resorted to biting his penis. The woman complained that her husband tried to choke her once all in the name of enhancing her arousal. He also had a habit of squeezing her breasts too tight, fingering her too aggressively, and sucking her neck intensely like a vampire. The man complained that his wife urinated on him once while orgasming, while the woman complained that her husband equally farted once during sex. The bickering continued and it was clear to Aina that the couple had increasingly become sexually frustrated and bored of each other. She found it contradictory that Christianity would preach against both divorce and premarital sex. What if the husband and wife were not sexually compatible? Wasn't divorce a reasonable solution? Was Christianity subtly promoting depression and resentment in marriages?

Another aspect of Christianity that confused Aina was the idea that masturbation was a sin against God. What if a person enjoyed being single but still craved sexual pleasure without having to need a sex partner? Wasn't masturbation the next best option?

The more Aina discovered about sexuality, the more skeptical she became of Christianity which was somewhat against sexual freedom. Still questioning Christianity, she found another confusing aspect of the religion to be the Eurocentric portrayal of Jesus as a White man with blue eyes. She often wondered where in history it was recorded that Jesus was White. She insisted that the portrayal of Jesus, the most powerful being, as White, was the highest level of White supremacy–if the Messiah was

White, then Whites were superior to all other races. She thought about interviewing some Catholics to ask how they would feel if the "Passion of Christ" movies were remade with a Black Jesus. She presumed that the movies would not sell because of racism. She wondered how many White Christians were willing to hang portraits of a Black Jesus on the walls of their homes.

Aina, upon finding more contradictory and illogical aspects of Christianity, began to wonder if God was real. She was eager to find out what life was truly about because everything she had been taught as a child had suddenly become confusing. She then knelt to pray to God, asking her to show herself in any surreal way, since God was supposedly omnipotent. Being a Black woman, Aina felt it right to equally depict her God as a Black woman in her mind. First, Aina challenged God, if she was truly real, to turn her shoe into a lizard. She waited ten minutes, but nothing happened. Her shoe was still a shoe. There was no lizard. Next, she challenged God to send a flying car across her window. She waited ten minutes again, but nothing happened. Aina was devastated. Had she been lied to her whole life about the existence of God? If God was not real, then what was life about?

The next day, an unusual thing happened. While researching articles online about the existence of God, she came across some spiritual audio books which looked interesting. She ordered them immediately and began to listen to them. Her favorites of these books were "The Happy Medium" and "Your Soul Purpose" by Kim Russo, a psychic medium. She also enjoyed "Conversations with God" by Neale Donald Walsch, "The Power of Now" by

Eckhart Tolle, "The Untethered Soul" by Michael Alan Singer, "Between Death and Life: Conversations with a Spirit" by Dolores Cannon, "The Instruction" by Ainslie MacLeod, and "How to Read the Akashic Records" by Linda Howe. Through these books, Aina began to understand that religion was simply a vessel towards actual spirituality–religion was spirituality tainted with human ideologies. The fundamental of every religion was unconditional love, modeled after the life of a spiritual master. For example, Christianity was modeled after the life of Jesus Christ; Islam was modeled after the life of Muhammad; and Buddhism was modeled after the life of Buddha. All these people were spiritual masters who simply taught unconditional love in different ways. As time went by, these teachings became tainted with human ideas to suit specific societal contexts.

The more spiritual audio books Aina listened to, the more she began to see that the world was an infinitely spiritual world, and that every soul was created to live infinite lives through multiple reincarnations. Each soul had a soul group to help them through their life's mission. This discovery of soul groups explained the feeling of meeting someone for the first time and feeling like you had known them forever. Their soul was probably in your soul group and had lived many lives with you, taking on different roles. For example, a soul who was your sister in one life could have chosen to be your mother in another life. She learned that every soul had picked its life path, including planet of birth, country of birth, name at birth, birthday, level of difficulty, family, etc. Aina also discovered that life was divided into either living in a state of fear or unconsciousness, or living in a state of love or consciousness. She finally started to see how her Christian upbringing had instilled a fear-based way of life. Christianity, as taught to her, preached about living to survive judgment day, and to avoid hell fire and the devil. Aina found these teachings to be ludicrous upon learning that hell, heaven, and the devil were all reflections of the states of one's soul. Heaven and hell were not destinations per se, but simply a soul operating from love or fear. Heaven was the peaceful state of a soul operating from unconditional love while hell was the state of a soul operating from fear. When a person's soul operated from fear, it exhibited negative emotions such as jealousy, anger, anxiety etc. Jealousy was a fear of losing something you already had; anger was a fear of being hurt; anxiety was a fear of losing control, etc. These negative fear-based emotions were what caused the uncomfortable feeling of being in hell. The devil was simply a fear-based influence. In other words, the devil was the ego.

Aina grew to understand that God was life itself. We were in God and God was in us. Contrary to religious teachings, God did not need to be worshiped because we were God. She likened this discovery of God to blood in one's body. If a person wanted to test the components of one's blood, only less than a pint of blood would be required. There would be no need to drain one's body of all of one's blood to carry out the test. The components of a small portion of one's blood would represent the rest of one's blood in one's body. Like God, we all together summed up to God while also being the same. Learning further, Aina also realized that there was no good or bad per se; everything was based on perspective. What people regarded as good and bad were simply opposite forces of life which balanced out each other. The idea of fulfilling one's life purpose meant that one had something to give to the world. To have something to give meant that there had to be someone on the receiving end. For example, doctors needed people to be sick for them to fulfill their purpose of providing healing. Lawyers needed faults in the legal system for them to fulfill their purpose of fighting for justice and fairness, and many more examples. Aina began to understand that the world was not broken, but rather was operating in perfect harmony, balancing out opposite forces in the form of "good" and "bad." The world was evolving cyclically, not linearly, in the sense that with new innovations came new problems. Every new effect had its counterbalance. Cyclical evolution explained the popular saying that "history had a way of repeating itself."

Aina, digging deeper into spirituality, also discovered meditation and the art of living in the moment. Understanding that life was infinite, she realized that there was no destination. Life was simply a series of present moments. What people regarded as death was merely a soul's transition into a new spiritual realm. She was fascinated to learn that psychics and mediums operated on the notion that the universe was solely energy whose vibrations could be manipulated to interpret spiritual messages. Aina thus laughed at the Bible's depiction of psychics and mediums as sinners and messengers of the devil. She became annoyed with religion for producing lazy thinkers. She was frustrated with the constraints that religion placed on people's abilities to reason intuitively and logically. Religion was the reason why the Catholic church was still against the use of contraceptives, knowing that poor family planning was one of the root causes of poverty. Religion was the reason why homosexuals around the world were still being persecuted. Religion was the reason why abortion, even when necessary to protect a mother's physical and mental health, was seen as a sin against God. Religion was the reason why patriarchy still existed in the world. Aina was utterly ashamed of some of her former Christian beliefs. She concluded that the world needed more spirituality and less religion. After listening to multiple spiritual audio books and rethinking all her beliefs, Aina realized that she had just undergone spiritual awakening. She was astonished to find out from "The Happy Medium" book that anyone undergoing spiritual awakening was likely to see numbers "1122" frequently popping up in their lives during that period. Aina's house number happened to be "11221" while three of her recent mails to her house seemed to have tracking numbers that began with or ended in "1122." This discovery was surreal for Aina. There was nothing left to convince her that spirituality was real.

After weeks of studying spirituality and finally denouncing her religion, Aina no longer believed in abstinence before marriage. She was completely sure that she was ready to embark on sexual relations with Tomiwa. Tomiwa, being non-religious, was open to sex before marriage as well.

Chapter 8

Aina and Tomiwa were both new to dating. As an intersex, Tomiwa had an abnormally large clitoris. Aina, aware of this attribute, wondered if she could be aroused by female genitalia. Before meeting Tomiwa, she had assumed she would end up dating and marrying a man. To begin their sexual escapade, Aina and Tomiwa decided to explore sex like they were lesbians. To educate themselves on lesbian sex, they visited a porn site to learn about different sex positions, and the best sex toys to use.

Aina and Tomiwa dated for a year before tying the knot. The couple got engaged and married the same week, which ended up being the most adventurous week of their lives together. The week started off with Aina flying them to Miami on a weekend. Tomiwa had no idea about the proposal Aina was planning. All they wanted to do was enjoy an overseas vacation with their girlfriend. Aina had planned to propose to Tomiwa on Miami beach on Wednesday. They landed at Miami International Airport on Sunday and proceeded to stay at a 5-star hotel. On Monday, they went on a boat cruise, toured art museums, visited amusement parks, and went clubbing at night. On Tuesday, they took yoga classes, did a city tour, and went kayaking. On Wednesday, Aina got the ring ready. She hoped the day would be perfect.

The proposal day started off with breakfast in bed, after which the couple made love for a bit, and then went to a spa. In the evening, Aina took Tomiwa to dinner at a lavish restaurant. The meal was set to be a five-course meal. Aina had planned with the waiter to serve the ring as the third course. When it was time for the third course, the waiter brought out a tray of two covered plates. He placed a covered plate each in front of Aina and Tomiwa. First, he opened Aina's plate and revealed a delicious looking meal. Tomiwa was jealous. The waiter then opened Tomiwa's plate slowly, and there sat the diamond ring. Tomiwa gasped for breath while staring at the ring, speechless. By that time, Aina was already on one knee. "You are the final piece to my puzzle. Let's make porn together for the rest of our lives. Will you marry me, Tomiwa?" said Aina. "Yes! Yes! Yes!" screamed Tomiwa as they both got up to hug each other. Everyone in the restaurant stood up to clap for the newly engaged couple.

When Aina and Tomiwa got back to the hotel room, Aina had another surprise for Tomiwa. She told Tomiwa she was going to the bathroom for a few minutes. Tomiwa undressed, getting ready to go to bed. By the time Aina came out of the bathroom, she was dressed in the sexiest red lingerie Tomiwa had ever seen. She turned on John Legend's "Tonight (Best You Ever Had)" song and began walking seductively towards the bed. As the newly engaged couple were about to begin making love, Tomiwa whispered into Aina's ear, "let's make porn baby." Aina laughed off their seductive whisper. She had no idea that Tomiwa meant every word they said. Apparently, Tomiwa had taken Aina's words at the dinner literally. As Tomiwa reached for their phone to begin recording, Aina leapt out of the bed in shock. Had the love of her life gone crazy? She sat at the edge of the bed to contemplate what they were about to do. Tomiwa persuaded Aina, insisting that the sex tape would be a fun way to commemorate their engagement. Only they would have access to the video. They would watch it every year on their engagement anniversary. After thirty minutes of persuasion, Aina finally agreed, and they had the dirtiest sex ever, recording themselves in every position possible. Their porn recording lasted hours, after which they collapsed into bed exhausted. The couple woke up late the next day. Still drained from the night before, they decided to order food in and spend the whole day watching television and making love at random times.

On Friday, Aina had a final surprise for Tomiwa. Unknown to Tomiwa, the night before, Aina had purchased two tickets to a Miami nudist beach. She presented a ticket to Tomiwa, asking them to get dressed for the trip. When they got to the beach, Aina undressed completely while Tomiwa was reluctant to take off their shorts. It took a bit of cajolery from Aina for Tomiwa to undress completely. Once the two were naked, they both ran into the water like five-year old kids on the beach for the first time. This exhilarating experience made Aina feel a sudden peak of liberation. She wondered if souls in other spiritual realms were naked or if they wore the same outfit from their earthly funeral. To continue the spontaneity, Aina proposed to Tomiwa that they get married right there on the nudist beach. Tomiwa laughed out loud before agreeing to the ludicrous plan. They asked a stranger to officiate the three-minute marriage ceremony while they stood there facing each other butt naked. After the short marriage ceremony, they proceeded to eat crawfish for lunch, after which they laid on their beach towels to get suntanned. As they laid there, Tomiwa slid their hand in between Aina's thighs and began to finger her. Within five seconds Aina let out a loud cry which startled Tomiwa. "Tommy! My v-jay-jay is on fire!" Tomiwa was confused. What could have suddenly caused the burning sensation in Aina's vulva? The answer finally clicked. It was the remnants of the peppery crawfish sauce left on his fingers. He had washed his hands thoroughly after lunch, but apparently, not all the sauce was gone. Aina, sitting with her legs spread wide open, wept silently as she washed her vulva with cool water. Their Miami trip was one for the books.

To end their wild trip, Aina and Tomiwa decided to get tattoos. Aina got a tattoo of the letter "T" on her left butt cheek while Tomiwa got a tattoo of the letter "A" on their right butt cheek. On their flight back to Lagos, they talked about their future together. Aina considered applying for Tomiwa to gain U.S. citizenship by marriage. Tomiwa was elated. Frustrated with Nigeria's discrimination against LGBTQIA+ culture, Tomiwa was willing to move to the U.S. with Aina whenever she was ready to relocate. Aina, however, wanted to remain in Nigeria for some time to keep growing her Fun Wa clothing brand and her Tiger's Den television show. Although, she still traveled to the U.S. every four months to ensure the smooth running of her Oyatosi fashion brand. She also began to consider expanding Fun Wa brand in America, and Oyatosi brand in Nigeria.

The couple also discussed the possibility of having kids in the future. Aware that they both had female external genitalia, they considered adoption or surrogacy. Tomiwa, however, proposed another idea of undergoing gender reassignment surgery to develop a penis. Tomiwa already had testes; all they needed was a penis to get Aina pregnant. Aina, fascinated by this idea, urged Tomiwa to explain further, how the reassignment surgery worked. Tomiwa was considering selecting one of two different surgeries: metoidioplasty or phalloplasty. Metoidioplasty was described as the surgical creation of a penis using the patient's existing genital tissue. It occurred by cutting the ligaments around the clitoris to release it from the pubis and give the shaft more length. Once released, the clitoris would start to resemble a baby penis. The doctor would then seal the vagina and enable the urethra to be able to come through the tiny hole in the small penis. Phalloplasty was described as the artificial construction or reconstruction of a penis. It involved the use of a grafted skin, typically taken from a donor site of the patient's body, such as the forearm, to form a neopenis. It also involved the creation of the urethra; creation of the scrotum; removal of the vagina; and placing of erectile and testicular implants.

Aina was excited about the idea of Tomiwa getting a penis but insisted on them revisiting the idea after at least a year. She worried that the gender reassignment surgery could affect Tomiwa mentally, long-term.

Aina, ready to launch a new controversial clothing line, deliberated over recent occurrences in her life which could influence the designs for her new line. Channeling the liberation she felt on the Miami nudist beach during her last vacation, she settled on nudity as a theme for her line. Before then, Aina had launched a clothing line that celebrated nudity through its patterns. This time, Aina wanted to release a provocative clothing line that exposed people's bodies, including their genitals. For women, she designed tops that had neck areas low enough not to cover their breasts or nipples. She also designed shorts, trousers, and skirts for women and men that were low enough to expose at least half of the person's butt crack and genital area. For the fashion show, she planned to begin by first showcasing photos of African ancestors who, before colonization, were typically almost naked all the time. Her goal was to send a message that she was bringing back African pre-colonial fashion. As soon as the clothing line was launched, as expected, all hell broke loose again in Lagos. During an interview on NTA news about her radical stance on nudity, Aina explained that children were never ashamed of their nakedness until their parents and the society taught them to be ashamed. Asserting that nudity was a natural way of life, she urged every Nigerian to embrace their inner child as well as the pre-colonial fashion of their ancestors.

One year later, Tomiwa finally decided on getting a phalloplasty. Aina in response, reproposed their old plan of launching a reality television show to share with Nigerians, their journey towards preparing for the surgery, undergoing the surgery, and starting a family. Tomiwa happily agreed to the plan. They were both willing to forfeit their privacy to debunk ignorance about intersex people's lives. Aina, already running Tiger's Den, knew the reality television space well enough, thus, launching her new series with Tomiwa was straightforward. As expected, once it was launched, the show got mixed reactions from Nigerians.

Months after Tomiwa had healed from their surgery, the couple was finally ready to have sexual intercourse. After their impromptu wedding in Miami, they had agreed to live together in Aina's mansion. To prepare for their special night, Tomiwa purchased romantic candles, rose petals, and two bottles of champagne, and came home early to prepare for Aina's arrival. They lit the candles in the bedroom; left a trail of rose petals from the front door, leading up the stairs, down to their bedroom; and set a bottle of champagne with two wine glasses on the bedside table.

Aina got home not too long after Tomiwa had finished setting the romantic scene. Tomiwa was sitting at the edge of the bed, wearing only underwear, and waiting for Aina. Aina, coming through the front door and seeing the trail of rose petals, gasped in astonishment. Following the trail, she already foresaw a romantic night coming. Aina was turned on. As soon as she saw Tomiwa, she ripped her clothes off, and the couple began making out aggressively. Once Tomiwa noticed Aina was heavily wet enough for penetration, they set out to go inside her. However, as soon as Tomiwa's penis touched Aina's vaginal opening, Aina began to weep uncontrollably. Tomiwa was confused. Wasn't Aina enjoying their intimacy? Tomiwa paused and consoled Aina, probing at the reason behind her sudden demeanor. Aina was confused as well. She did not know why she was crying. All she knew was that she could not proceed with the sexual intercourse. The couple decided to try again the next day, and throughout the rest of the week, but Aina nevertheless wept every single time. Frustrated with this strange occurrence in their marriage, they both decided to try out couples' therapy.

"Aina, have you considered reflecting on the history of all your sexual experiences before meeting Tomiwa? It seems to me like you may be dealing with trauma from a past sexual experience, which would explain the sudden weeping during sex. I've dealt with similar cases with former clients," said the therapist. "I have kissed only two boys before Tomiwa, but nothing beyond kissing. Tomiwa is the first person I have ever attempted to have sex with," responded Aina. The therapist looked concerned. "Were you ever groped as a young girl? Or were you sexually assaulted in any way?" asked the therapist. "Never," responded Aina. "Is there anything, no matter how small, that makes you nervous about having sexual intercourse with Tomiwa? If you need privacy, we could ask Tomiwa to step out for a bit," said the therapist. "Tomiwa can stay. There's nothing I can think of. I've been looking forward to sexual intercourse with them for months," responded Aina. "Based on your answers, it seems like you may be dealing with trauma from a past life. Have you heard of past life regression?" asked the therapist. "Yes, I believe so. My best friend told me about it some time ago, but I never thought to undergo it because I didn't think I had any phobias or anxieties to look into," answered Aina. "Well, now you do. I'll refer you to a past life regression therapist who would help you decipher the root of this trauma. Let me know how it goes," concluded the therapist.

The following week, Aina visited a past life regression therapist as recommended by her therapist. "Before you begin, I need you to know something. I recently read blogs about people who developed new trauma after having to relive oppressive moments in their past lives. I don't want that to happen to me. Will that happen to me?" asked Aina. "Past life regression therapy is not an easy process. Looking into a traumatic event in your past life will be uncomfortable, but in the long run, it has proven to help heal lingering traumas in people's present day lives. Basically, it is left to you to be courageous enough to confront your deepest fears to live a more peaceful life. You're in good hands darling," insisted the therapist, squeezing Aina's hand. "Trust me, it is not as bad as you think."

The hypnosis began with Aina counting down and breathing slowly. The therapist then began asking Aina a series of questions to figure out where she was and what was happening. After fifteen minutes of the ongoing hypnosis, Aina woke up. The hypnosis had taken her back to a time in her previous life when she was gang raped by eight boys and beaten to death. The rape took place when she was twelve years old and had just begun menstruation. In that past life, her first experience with sexual intercourse was via rape, which explained why she had struggled with letting Tomiwa penetrate her in her present life. The therapist, empathizing with Aina, immediately recommended follow-up sessions to help her work through the trauma.

Chapter 9

In her third year of working as a full-time neuroscience researcher, Udoka began to attend conferences and networking events on behalf of the company she worked for. Once, she attended a conference where top neurologists and neurosurgeons were to hold panel discussions on the adoption of a new cutting-edge medical technology. After the informative session, Udoka hurried to engage one-on-one with the panelists. Her plan was to introduce herself and the firm she worked for, get their contacts, and then leave. However, she ended up having a lengthy conversation with one of the panelists, Dr. Justin Brown. Dr. Brown was a middle-aged man who although was handicapped, happened to be a recognized leading neurosurgeon in America. Udoka, who naturally gravitated towards unorthodoxy, was immediately intrigued by Dr. Brown. Talking to him, she was even more drawn towards his warmth and openness. He willingly talked about his background and his unique experience as a physically disabled neurosurgeon. The two professionals, upon learning that they both had Nigerian backgrounds, were eager to connect as friends outside of the conference.

The evening after the conference, Udoka and Dr. Brown met up for dinner. Dr. Brown talked about growing up in Nigeria, including being adopted by African American parents at age ten. He became handicapped at age six after being shot in the neck by some cultists who had broken into his parents' home. His parents were killed in cold blood. Dr. Brown later learned that the cultists were sent by a notorious politician whom Dr. Brown's birth parents had exposed publicly for corruption. His parents were radical journalists who had set up a firm, primarily focused on exposing misdemeanors within the government and wealthy corporations in Nigeria. Dr. Brown's birth parents began dating while they were journalism students at Lagos University and got married two years after graduation. While at Lagos University, they had both been dedicated members of the university's student journalism club, dedicating their leisure hours towards uncovering hidden criminal incidents among students and professors. Dr. Brown's birth mother became feared by teachers on campus after she exposed one of her professors for attempted rape, leading to his expulsion. She published a scathing article in the campus newsletter which surprisingly got the attention of BBC Africa. Before this incident, Lagos University had been infamous for exhibiting a laissez-faire attitude towards interactions between professors and students. The university administration upon being investigated by BBC Africa, pledged to prioritize maintaining decorum on campus from then on.

After his parents were killed and no extended family member was willing to take him in, Dr. Brown was sent to an orphanage where he lived until he was adopted four years later. His adoptive parents were an African American couple who had relocated to Nigeria. While in America, they had taken an ancestry DNA test that showed that they had Nigerian heritage. To connect with their origins, they decided to move to Nigeria for a couple of years. After struggling in vain to conceive children, they settled on adoption, which was how they found Dr.

Brown. Once the adoption process was completed, the family lived in Nigeria for six more years before relocating to America. Dr. Brown was sixteen years old when he arrived in the United States. His adoptive parents were both doctors who were wealthy enough to enroll him into a private high school that catered towards physically disabled students. After being shot in the neck at age six, he was left paralyzed in both legs. Dr. Brown excelled through high school, and eventually chose to go into medicine like his adoptive parents. He studied neuroscience as his pre-medical undergraduate degree, before enrolling into a medical school that accommodated physically disabled students.

With adequate accommodations put in place for him in medical school, Dr. Brown remained a high-performing student. However, when it was time to pick a specialty, his family, except his parents, were shocked when he picked surgery. For years, they had admired his dedication to striving for academic excellence despite being disabled, but surgery to them seemed to be an over-ambitious choice. "Justin, are you pulling our legs? Don't you realize you will need to stand for long hours in the operating room? I don't think I have ever seen a surgeon perform operations while in a wheelchair," lamented Dr. Brown's cousin during a Thanksgiving dinner. "Haven't you heard of standing wheelchairs? You all should check them out online," replied Justin. "Wow! I had no idea that these existed! Why haven't I seen you in one?" asked Dr. Brown's aunt. "I've just never needed one, but I'll begin to use them once I begin my surgical rotations," responded Justin. Dr. Brown's parents, who were doctors, already knew about standing wheelchairs being used by doctors in hospitals, and thus laughed at their family's ignorance. Dr. Brown eventually opted for neurosurgery, which he increasingly excelled at over the years.

In addition to bonding over both having neuroscience backgrounds, Udoka was fascinated by Dr. Brown's story of endurance. When Udoka told her story of being a former sex slave, Dr. Brown was equally in awe of her strength and perseverance. The two friends were clearly survivors. The conversation took a more interesting turn when they decided to dabble into each other's romantic lives. Udoka, to Dr. Brown's surprise, had not dated anyone ever since she escaped slavery. After being forced to have sex with random men for five years, upon her release, she had decided to pour all her energy into catching up on her education. Dr. Brown, on the other hand, had dated multiple women but had never been married. For a long time, he could not understand why so many women were interested in him, considering his disability; however, he soon learned that the world still had people who were attracted to inner beauty. Without Udoka needing to ask, he assured her that he had a healthy sex life despite his condition, generally with the help of sexual medication. Before embarking on sexual relationships, Dr. Brown had enrolled in sex surrogacy which was a therapeutic process designed to help people become more comfortable with sex. In the program, he was taught convenient ways to have sex as a disabled person. His successful completion of the program was what boosted his confidence during sex with his girlfriends. He soon realized that although he could have erections, he was unable to ejaculate or orgasm. Fortunately, this issue was not a problem for Dr. Brown or his girlfriends. In fact, Dr. Brown's inability to orgasm was an amazing thing for his girlfriends because it meant they had no time limit around climaxing. Seeing his girlfriends orgasm during sex was enough to keep Dr. Brown aroused. The only reason his former relationships had ended was because he was not interested in getting married or having children, which was a deal breaker for the women.

After three months of getting to know each other, Udoka and Dr. Brown began dating. Udoka was not keen on getting married or having kids, hence, Dr. Brown seemed perfect for her. Despite his handicap, she found him to be incredibly handsome, while also falling in love with his decency. Although Dr. Brown was twenty years older than Udoka, he was still young at heart and adventurous, which Udoka loved about him. With Udoka and Dr. Brown residing in Houston, Texas and Baltimore, Maryland respectively, the relationship ended up being long-distance. The couple however managed to make it work with daily video calls and two days of vacation every month. Dr. Brown was a wealthy surgeon, and thus was able to afford their extravagant vacations. Udoka's best part of her vacations with her boyfriend was having to sit on his lap while he rolled his wheelchair down a free pathway, into the sunset. She would let the breeze blow her hair, while resting her face on his chest. They were so in love. Whenever they were together, she would happily assist him with certain activities such as getting into the shower, getting into the car, getting into bed, etc. Sex was amazing for Udoka. Dr. Brown would commonly tease her about waking up everyone in the hotel with her loud moans.

One year into her romantic relationship, Udoka began to think about the next step in her career. She had enjoyed amazing years as a researcher in childhood development disorders, but was ready to explore a new area, still within childhood development. She contemplated stepping back into psychology, but this time, coupled with technology. During a brainstorming session, she remembered an inspirational documentary she had watched some years back, called "Life, Animated" which shed light on how an autistic child relied on watching only cartoons at home to help him understand the way the world worked. Using a similar idea, she decided that her next career would focus on creating ethnic animated movies and computer games primarily for African and African American children. Udoka was disappointed that the only mainstream cartoon shows and computer games she was aware of, were typically westernized. She wanted Black children to start early to see themselves and their culture represented in the animated shows they watched and computer games they played. In her shows, she planned to depict topics such as body positivity, inclusion for mentally and physically disabled children, feminism, cultural languages and idiosyncrasies, and other matters which she felt would help kids develop into confident and compassionate individuals.

To prepare for this new career path, she concluded on getting a master's degree in computer graphics and game technology from Pennsylvania University.

Chapter 10

After discovering that her fear of losing her virginity was associated with trauma from being gang-raped in her past life, Aina spent the next few months undergoing psychotherapy. Thankfully, Tomiwa was eventually able to penetrate her, and within two weeks, Aina became pregnant with their first child. To celebrate her pregnancy, she spent her first and second trimesters designing genderless, edgy kids' clothes. Her goal with this new line was to encourage parents to start early to instill freedom of gender expression in their kids. Tomiwa, on the other hand, was ready for a career change. They had recently watched Kanye West's documentary, "Jeen-Yuhs," and was inspired by his courage to push boundaries in the music and fashion industry. Kanye had started off as a talented record producer but proved his doubters wrong by also becoming a prominent rapper and fashion designer. Tomiwa had started off as an audio engineer but had begun to consider becoming a rapper as well. Inspired by intelligent rappers such as Kendrick Lamar and J. Cole, they began writing intellectual rap lyrics focused on social justice issues, life as an intersex, Nigerian culture, LGBTQIA+ culture, love, depression, and many other matters dear to their heart.

To launch their career, Tomiwa connected with record producers whom they had worked with in the past, as an audio engineer. After receiving multiple rejections, they finally got approved by a prominent music producer who was willing to take a chance with them. The producer, impressed with the depth and rawness of Tomiwa's lyrics, signed them immediately. Other producers had been too nervous about the possibility of Tomiwa's LGBTQIA+ affiliation affecting album sales and business deals. Tomiwa was just grateful to have someone who believed in them. They soon began recording sessions for their debut album.

    Within five months, Tomiwa completed their debut album, released it, and began brainstorming concert ideas. As expected, their debut album received mixed feedback from Nigerians. Some appreciated the intensity and edginess of the lyrics and sound; some appreciated Tomiwa for embodying non-binary fashion in their music videos; some denigrated Tomiwa for "looking like a freak" in the videos; among other commentaries. Meanwhile, for concerts, Tomiwa came up with a fundraiser idea for historical sites in Nigeria. They decided on partnering with sites which were struggling financially to preserve Nigerian cultural heritage. Tomiwa, upon performing at these sites, would pay them the amount that would have otherwise been spent on a general mainstream venue typically used by other music artists. The sites they had in mind included the National War Museum, the Slave Museum, National Museum Lagos, Freedom Park Lagos, and so on. In the early stages of Tomiwa's concerts, the turnout at sites outside Lagos were initially low, but eventually grew as they garnered more fans nation-wide. Tomiwa's fundraiser plan proved successful in the long run. However, once Aina delivered their beautiful son, they both took a year-long leave to focus solely on raising their child.

    Aina's mother came over to help with taking care of the baby, but also brought along some retrograde ideas of how to care for a newborn. She insisted that the baby should be fed infant formula instead of breastmilk, believing that breastmilk was not adequate for a male child. She then advised Aina to introduce solid foods into the baby's diet as early as possible, to enable him to gain strength quickly. Aina's mother believed that breastmilk was only meant for female babies, while male babies needed more solid foods to cater to their higher energy expenditure. She was also certain that colostrum was dirty milk. Aina and Tomiwa were skeptical of this new information considering that the nurses at their hospital had insisted on breastmilk being the best option for their newborn. Nevertheless, Aina's mother somehow convinced them that Nigerian hospitals tended to make wrong medical decisions. Aina eventually agreed with her mother after reading articles online about the medical failings of some Nigerian hospitals. The most alarming incident was how a young woman had contracted HIV from being transfused with contaminated blood at a Nigerian hospital.

Aina began to feed her son formula as advised by her mother, and within a month, introduced yam porridge into his diet. Regrettably, within one week, the child became sick. At the hospital, the doctor diagnosed his illness to be bowel blockage and an allergic reaction to the formula. Aina was devastated. The doctor explained that the baby's diet was what caused the illness, insisting that breastfeeding was the best option for infant feeding. After that day, Aina refused to take any more parenting advice from her mother. Taking a keen interest in the importance of breastfeeding, she began to read up articles online about the topic. Aina, upon learning that the colostrum of a nursing mother was the most nutritious part of her breast milk, mocked her mother's ignorant view that it was "dirty milk." She was also fascinated to learn that there was an economic component to breastfeeding–breast milk, which was more nutritious than infant formula made from cow milk, contained core nutrients that helped to reduce the onset of diseases in infants. A reduction in the onset of diseases translated into lower rehospitalization rates, and lower rehospitalization rates meant lower healthcare costs. She was alarmed to find out that inadequate breastfeeding was costing the Nigerian economy about twenty-one billion dollars per year. Reading further, Aina learned that companies that provided lactation support programs for their female employees tended to get a return on investment of three dollars to every dollar invested in the program. Companies with lactation programs typically had a high retention rate of their childbearing employees who were also less likely to take absences to care for their sick babies. Less absenteeism translated into higher revenue for these companies.

After a year of intense parenting, the couple decided to return to being creatives. They hired enough nannies to assist them at home, while they deliberated innovative ways to grow their careers. Aina thought about combining some of her fashion shows with Tomiwa's concerts to increase the quantity and diversity of attendees. She planned to then record these shows and transform them into documentaries on Netflix to generate more income. Tomiwa contemplated organizing annual LGBTQIA+ music festivals with special appearances from international LGBTQIA+ inspired music artists such as Lil

Nas, Todrick Hall, Janelle Monáe, Big Freedia etc. Inspired by RuPaul, an American drag queen, they were also willing to add drag shows as part of the festival. Tomiwa was pro Pan-Africanism, and thus always envisioned partnerships with international Black artists.

As Tomiwa's musical career grew, they considered more ways to empower LGBTQIA+ culture via ideas such as partnering with sponsors to create an LGBTQIA+ version of "Big Brother Nigeria." Big Brother Nigeria was a reality television show in which contestants lived in an isolated house and competed for a hefty cash prize at the end of the show by avoiding being evicted by viewers. Tomiwa also thought about launching a Nigerian version of "Queer Eye" television show to highlight positive ways that LGBTQIA+ Nigerians were contributing to societal development. Queer Eye was an American show that followed five queer lifestyle experts as they forged relationships with lay Americans who needed makeovers in areas such as grooming, fashion, food and wine, interior design, among others. Over a span of five years, Tomiwa successfully implemented these ideas with the help of local and international sponsors.

"Babe! Wake up! Wake up!" screamed Tomiwa at three a.m. one morning. "It's our sex tape! It's online! Aina! Wake up right now!" Aina, still groggy, peeked at Tomiwa's phone, and her heart started to pound. Minutes before then, Tomiwa had merely woken up to use the restroom. Before jumping back into bed, they had decided to glance at Twitter for a few minutes only to find their sex tape being retweeted by multiple accounts. The couple was being trolled again on social media. During their years of becoming cultural icons in Nigeria, they had become targets of constant intrusion from strangers. Their leaked sex tape was the peak of privacy invasion they had suffered so far. Tomiwa had stored the couple's sex tape from their engagement night on their iCloud, but apparently it had been hacked. To contain the situation as fast as possible, they made emergency calls that morning to figure out how to take down the tape from all sites. They were willing to pay any amount of money to end the embarrassment. The couple remained frantic while waiting on responses. To escape public ridicule, they decided to keep low profiles until the issue was resolved. After a month of being lowkey with no progress of removing the tape, Aina made a daring decision to flip the situation in their favor. Her plan was to upload the tape on as many porn sites as possible, to earn an income from it. Tomiwa was not on board with this new plan at first. However, after careful contemplation, and a recall of their favorite quote, "Life does not happen to you, it happens for you," they finally agreed to the plan. Aina, who was happy to see Tomiwa snap out of their victim mentality, began searching for porn sites that paid well enough. She was ecstatic upon finding sites that were willing to pay ten thousand dollars and above per a million views on each porn video. The social media trolling continued nevertheless, only that this time, the couple was now channeling the humiliation into income. In subsequent interviews relating to her sex tape, Aina proudly stated that sex, which brought so much pleasure to humans, was an activity to be celebrated publicly not shamed.

Aina and Tomiwa continued to deliberate new ways to support Nigerian youth. Aina's new idea was to launch a show called "Nigeria's Next in Fashion," which would be a seasonal competition among budding fashion designers in Nigeria. The competitors would be instructed to design their best looks based on dictated themes, within a specified time frame. The winner would then be awarded a hefty cash prize to grow their business, while receiving mentorship from Aina. Buying from this same idea, Aina encouraged Tomiwa to also launch "Nigeria's Next in Rap," which would be a seasonal competition to find the next best talented rapper within Nigeria. The winner would receive a cash prize and would be signed to a record label which was willing to partner with Tomiwa on the project. Tomiwa, ecstatic about both ideas, added that it would be cool to launch both projects at the same time, as a power couple. The couple spent the rest of the year working to implement these ideas.

Chapter 11

Udoka began her master's degree at Pennsylvania University, happy to finally live closer to her boyfriend, Dr. Brown. She was now only a two-hour drive away from him, which meant that they could see each other every weekend. Like her undergraduate experience, Udoka decided to take advantage of both academic and extracurricular opportunities at her new school. She joined the African Caribbean Student Association, Black Student Union, and applied to become a graduate resident advisor (GRA). Udoka was excited about the graduate resident advisor position because of the opportunity to mentor first-year students, while overseeing their housing accommodations on campus. Looking back at her first year in college, she remembered her struggle with settling into campus, coupled with pursuing a double major. As a result, Udoka was eager to support her first-year residents as much as possible. She was also particularly concerned about the new international students who were likely to experience culture shock during their first few months. Another reason she was excited about the GRA position was its guarantee of free housing offered by the university's housing department. The GRAs upon being hired were each to be offered a free room and meal plan to live and dine among the residents whom they were placed in charge of. Udoka was grateful for any opportunity to cut down tuition and accommodation fees.

Upon receiving the GRA job offer, Udoka began to plan out activities for her first-year residents. She thought about incorporating an alternating buddy system that matched a resident with another resident for a month.

Each buddy pair would then be encouraged to hang out together for the month and hopefully form close ties. During floor meetings, the buddies would each give a short fun presentation on what activities they did together and what they learned about each other. She was confident that this idea would help the residents make friends quickly since they were all new to campus. She also thought about organizing a fun costume gala at the end of each semester; potluck to try out dishes from different ethnicities and cultures; fields trips; movie nights; and other fun activities to foster camaraderie among her residents.

Udoka moved in two weeks earlier than her residents, to undergo GRA training. Once school resumed officially, she spent move-in day welcoming and guiding her residents to their assigned rooms. Once everyone was settled in, she introduced herself to her new residents, encouraging them to contact her about any issue that they needed help with. She then gave them a tour of the residential building, dictated residential rules, and summarized all the activities that she had planned out for them for the semester.

Udoka spent the rest of the semester juggling schoolwork and GRA duties. In addition to implementing bonding activities for her residents, she found herself having to settle disputes, report cases of misdemeanors to campus security, guide troubled residents towards proper handling of their personal matters, etc. Once, she had a case of a student whom she found cutting her wrist while studying in one of the residence study rooms. The student, remembering that Udoka had a psychology background, decided to share details of a deeply personal traumatic event which was causing her depression, hoping that Udoka would help her through it. Joyce was an eighteen-year-old Zimbabwean international student who was from a wealthy, but abusive home. Growing up in Zimbabwe, her father had sexually molested her multiple times, and threatened to kill her if she ever reported to anyone. Her mother had died before her third birthday, leading her father to marry a woman whom Joyce suspected to be a gold digger, pretending to be in love with her father. Her stepmother, who never cared for her, was the wrong person to discuss her problems with. Joyce was not close to any of her extended family members because her father had prohibited her early on, from associating with any of them. He had convinced himself that keeping his family at a distance would prevent them from becoming financially dependent on him, considering that he was the wealthiest of them all. Joyce was homeschooled up to her twelfth grade and locked up in a mansion her whole life, causing her to become socially awkward. She resorted to relying solely on her puppy for affection, after trying unsuccessfully to befriend the maids and cooks that worked in her father's mansion. Joyce's father had threatened to fire them if they ever got close to Joyce. All his employees feared him. Joyce soon learned that her father's plan was to isolate her as much as possible from the world, while he continued molesting her. Joyce was only able to escape from the mansion after her father was arrested for fraud. To get away from Zimbabwe and continue with her education, she applied to colleges in America and was eventually admitted into Pennsylvania University to study architecture. To fund her education, Joyce was lucky to find out that her father had set up a trust fund for her which she could access only after she turned eighteen. Unfortunately, although Joyce had achieved freedom for herself, she was still dealing with trauma from being sexually molested by her father. She felt worthless and habitually contemplated suicide.

Halfway through listening to Joyce's story, Udoka began to weep. Her resident's story had triggered a traumatic memory of her experience as a former sex slave. She could relate to Joyce's feeling of worthlessness. She shared with Joyce, her trauma of being a former sex slave, and how she was able to recover emotionally after undergoing therapy for a year. The next day, she accompanied Joyce to book a session with a therapist at the campus health clinic. This experience was one of the most profound of all Udoka's encounters as a GRA.

By her second year as a graduate student, Udoka began to prepare for her master's capstone project. Inspired by her experience with Joyce, she chose to prepare an hour-long animated movie that focused on teaching kids about consent, respect for their bodies, ways to identify pedophiles, and emergency numbers to call if they ever encountered a pedophile. After her graduation, she moved to Baltimore to find a job as a computer animator. Dr. Brown and Udoka, elated that they were finally able to work in the same city, decided to move in together. After three years of living together as a couple, Udoka began to have sudden flashbacks about the baby she had given up during her time as a sex slave. She kept having horrible dreams about the child being sold into slavery, escaping after ten years, and eventually ending up living with callous foster parents. Udoka consulted a psychic about the meaning of her vivid dreams and was told that her child was trying to communicate with her. Her son, who had lived a life of misery since birth, frequently cried out to his birth mother at night, to come back for him. He believed that her spirit could hear his cry. He was in dire need of a mother's love. Udoka accepted the psychic's recommendation and set out to find her son. She was nervous about the journey because of the fear that reuniting with her child could possibly bring back old traumatic memories of her slavery experience. Nevertheless, she remained determined to put an end to her nightmares and her sudden strange feeling of incompleteness. Udoka had developed a sudden void in her that she was convinced could only be filled from reuniting with her son. Dr. Brown, who had never wanted kids, surprisingly was on board with Udoka finding her lost child. He was so in love with Udoka that he inadvertently often found himself feeling all her emotions. When she was sad, he was sad, and when she was happy, he was happy. His relationship with Udoka was the deepest and most frightening he had ever been in. He was convinced that Udoka was his soulmate.

To begin the journey towards finding her child, Udoka contacted the Los Angeles FBI agents who had rescued her from sex slavery, pleading with them to assist her in the search. The agents, after looking into the case, informed her that the brothel managers they had arrested had also been running a baby factory. They supposed that Udoka's baby had been sent to that same factory. However, after shutting down the baby factory, the rescued babies had been placed in foster care. The FBI proposed that Udoka's baby could have been among those sent to foster care, except that some of the babies had already been sold into slavery before the demolition of the factory. In other words, Udoka's child could have been placed into foster care, or could have been sold into slavery. Udoka was distressed. To proceed, she decided to rely on the details of her dream, which the psychic had convinced her was a clue to finding her son. Recalling her dream, she saw that her son was sold into slavery, but was rescued years later, and placed into foster care. Thus, Udoka's next plan was to seek the help of foster care authorities to search for her son within their system. The search seemed impossible at first because Udoka had no idea what her child's current name was, or what he looked like as a grown kid. Udoka was frustrated but found hope again when the FBI came up with a new idea. They informed her that after shutting down the baby factory, they had confiscated all information about the operations of the factory. Within these included photos of all the babies who had been bred within the factory. If Udoka could identify her baby's photo, then the FBI would interrogate the former factory managers in prison to figure out who they had sold the baby to. Udoka fortunately still remembered the exact features of her baby's looks. She successfully identified the baby's photo, and the search continued. After hours of cross-examination from the FBI, the former factory managers finally released the passwords to hidden documents detailing whom Udoka's baby had been sold to. Interestingly, the person who had purchased the child also happened to have been arrested years later and was currently locked up in prison. Under his management, for ten years, Udoka's son had served as a sex slave for pedophilic clients, before being rescued and placed in a foster home. The man informed the FBI of the child's slave name which was probably also being used in the foster care system. Udoka was grateful to be one step closer to finding her son.

It took about a week for the FBI to track down Udoka's son within the foster care system. The day mother and child were to meet up, Udoka could hardly stop trembling. Dr. Brown had flown down from Baltimore to Los Angeles to witness the reunion of his girlfriend and her lost child. He too was trembling. None of them could deny the intensity of that moment. Once Udoka saw her grown child, she burst into tears as they hugged tightly, refusing to let go of each other. "Mommy, I always knew you would come back for me. I used to cry out to you every night, and I knew deep within me that you were listening," said her son. "Yes! I heard you baby! I heard your cry through my dreams! I love you so much! I am so sorry for everything you've been through," responded Udoka. By this time, Dr. Brown had joined in to hug mother and son. Udoka proceeded to expedite the adoption process for her son. Once it was complete, she decided it was time to give him a new dignified name. Udoka renamed her child "Nkem," meaning "mine" in Igbo, and for his last name, he took her maiden name, "Ike." Since Udoka and Dr. Brown were still unmarried, and Dr. Brown was not Nkem's biological father, they decided that Nkem would refer to Dr. Brown by his first name, "Justin." Nkem moved into Udoka and Dr. Brown's home, and the family lived happily together. Nkem was enrolled in the best school in Baltimore and was showered with constant parental love which he had been deprived of as a child.

After five years of living with her family in Baltimore, Udoka felt it was time for her to give back to Nigeria. She was ready to move back home for some time, and she wanted her family to come with her. Her new plan initially seemed inconvenient for Dr. Brown, who was enjoying his time as a highly paid, respected neurosurgeon in Baltimore. However, after weighing all options, he fancied the idea of moving back as well, having been away from Nigeria for decades. He was excited to reconnect with his roots but was mostly eager to bring innovative medicine into Nigeria. The family spent the rest of the year preparing to relocate, while Nkem gushed to his friends about moving to "Africa." Before relocating, Udoka, however, wanted to give back one last time to America. She came up with an idea to set up an animal shelter for rescued animals in a low-income area of Baltimore. Her plan was for the rescued animals to then be used as playmates for special needs kids in the area. During her time as a researcher in the childhood development disorders space, she had learned that providing special needs children with pets was an important way to enhance emotional support for these kids. Using donations from local philanthropists, Udoka implemented her plan, and hired volunteers to manage the shelter, and report its progress to her while she was in Nigeria. Udoka planned to visit the shed during her seasonal visits to the U.S., to ensure its smooth running.

Dr. Brown's plan, upon relocating to Nigeria, was to set up a renowned hospital that would be known for implementing cutting-edge medicine. He was excited to partner with doctors who were willing to help train talent within the country. Alongside his hospital, Dr. Brown also focused on establishing the first neuroscience research center in Nigeria. To concentrate on running his hospital, he appointed Udoka to be the chief operating officer (COO) of the center. Aina was the first investor to put money into the development of the research center. She seemed certain about the huge impact it was going to have on Nigeria's healthcare sector. Udoka, in addition to running the research center, also worked on producing more animated films for kids, and writing children's books. Through Aina's help, she connected with Mo Abudu, a Nigerian media mogul, to help launch her films.

After working in the Nigerian film industry for a while, Udoka began to consider other areas of film production. Being passionate about social issues in the country, she decided to try out making documentaries. Her first documentary was on the struggles of Nigerian doctors within a failing healthcare system. Having a husband who had firsthand knowledge about these inefficiencies gave her enough insight into what issues to highlight. She spent months shadowing doctors across Nigeria and documenting their most pressing obstacles within the healthcare system. Udoka was tired of vague answers such as "corruption" whenever she asked a lay Nigerian what issues the country was facing. She wanted Nigerians to know the exact problems going on in the country to protest for exact solutions to be implemented. For activism to be successful, there had to be a specific cause with specific demands. Hence, the end goal of her documentary was to bring to light, specific problems Nigerian doctors were facing, to help Nigerian youth streamline what demands were the most important to highlight during protests.

Chapter 12

Aina and Udoka, alongside their families, generally took vacations together, while in Lagos. As Aina got to know Dr. Brown on a personal level, she grew to respect his tenacity and brilliance. She particularly admired his fashion sense, curious to know if he had the same shopping experience as a non-disabled person. Did he ever struggle to find well-fitted clothes? Did his disability affect his body proportions? Dr. Brown, impressed with Aina's curiosity, explained that his legs had shrunk because of his injury. He assumed that the biological explanation for this occurrence was that immobility typically caused the cartilage to shrink and stiffen. As a young disabled boy, he had struggled to find well-fitted pants, thus he usually resorted to wearing oversized pants. However, as he became more financially stable, he began to purchase custom-made pants that were tailored to fit his actual size. Aina, fascinated by how much she was learning from him, asked for tips on how to make her clothing brand more inclusive for disabled people. Dr. Brown responded, advising her to incorporate people with disabilities into all stages of product designs. He also encouraged her to design adaptive, fashionable clothing to fit body proportions and enable ease in wearing, and to put disabled people on the runway during fashion shows. He mentioned that some ways to design adaptive clothing included using snaps instead of buttons; adding magnetic closures to a button-down shirt but leaving the buttons for aesthetic purpose; and designing clothes that could be worn while sitting, and easy to put on unassisted. Aina was overjoyed with these ideas. As soon as she returned to work that week, she began to implement them into her new clothing line.

    The more time Udoka and Aina's families spent together, the more they influenced each other's lifestyles and career progressions. Aina's son became a child actor and was hired on multiple occasions to feature in Udoka's animated films as a voice actor. Udoka's son, Nkem, worked for Aina for a few years to learn pattern designing, and eventually became an interior designer. Dr. Brown and Tomiwa collaborated on a project to introduce music therapy into mental health facilities in Nigeria. Udoka and Aina remained the best of friends, challenging each other at every chance to grow into gutsy changemakers transforming Nigeria one day at a time.

Special thanks to my friends and family who provided constructive feedback on the initial drafts of this book.

Chinelo Ibekwe is a Nigerian currently pursuing an MSE in data science at the University of Pennsylvania. She has a BSc in chemical engineering from the University of Mississippi, where she pledged Delta Sigma Theta Sorority, Inc. In addition to pursuing a career in technology innovation, Chinelo is passionate about highlighting pressing social issues in the world via creative writing, oil paintings, and mass media. She believes that spirituality is the foundation of all solutions to the world's problems.

Made in the USA
Columbia, SC
19 February 2023